DIRTY MOVIES

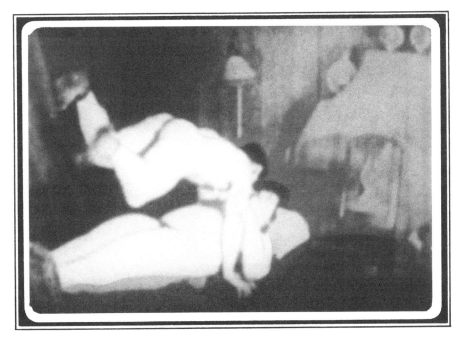

CHELSEA HOUSE

DIRTY MOVIES
An Illustrated History of the Stag Film
1915-1970

Al Di Lauro and Gerald Rabkin
with an introductory essay by
Kenneth Tynan

CHELSEA HOUSE
New York, London   1976

PROJECT EDITOR: DEBORAH WEISS
ART DIRECTOR: SUSAN LUSK
PRODUCTION ASSISTANT: LAURIE LIKOFF
TYPOGRAPHER: P. BARONNE AND SONS LTD.

Library of Congress Catalog Number 76-43040
ISBN 0-87754-046-2

Distributed by Whirlwind Books, New York

CHELSEA HOUSE PUBLISHERS

Harold Steinberg, Publisher   Andrew Norman, President
A Division of Chelsea House Educational Communications, Inc.
70 West 40th Street, New York, N.Y. 10018

Dedication
To Tom Rapkin (1930-60)

THE AUTHORS ARE INDEBTED to John Gagnon, Maurice Charney, Roger Greenspun, and Al LaValley for their valuable suggestions regarding the manuscript. Also, our appreciation to the staff of the Institute for Sex Research, Bloomington, Indiana, particularly Paul Gebhard, Cornelia Christenson, William Dellenback, William Simon, Eugene Slabaugh, and George Huntington, for their cooperation with Mr. Rabkin when he worked in their film archives during the 1960s. And, special thanks to Deborah Weiss for her helpful editing.

TABLE OF CONTENTS

Acknowledgments, 8

Foreword, 11
      "In Praise of Hard Core"
        by Kenneth Tynan

Dirty Movies
      A Pandora's Box of Definitions, 25
      The Rise of Pornography, 35
      Enter the Stag, 41
      Wonders of the Unseen World, 52
      'Bye, 'Bye, Miss American Pie, 59
      International Vistas: French, English, No Greek, 75
      Themes and Variations, 91
      End of an Era, 105

Bibliography, 121

Filmography, 125

IN PRAISE OF HARD CORE

Kenneth Tynan

IT'S ALWAYS PLEASANT to see prudery knocked, and whenever I read articles by fellow-intellectuals in defence of pornography, I do my best to summon up a cheer. Lately, however, the heart has gone out of my hurrahs. The old adrenalin glow has waned. And now that I've analysed a number of recent anti-censorship tracts, I think I know why. *The writers are cheating.* A whiff of evasiveness, even of outright hypocrisy, clings to their prose: too much is left unspoken, or unadmitted. Their arguments, when you look at them closely, shift on the quicksands of timidity. On the surface, a fearless libertarian has come forth to do battle with the forces of reaction. But between the lines he is usually saying something like this:

(a) I hate censorship in all its forms, but that doesn't mean that I actually like pornography.

(b) In fact, I don't even approve of it, except when I can call it 'erotic writing' and pass it off as literature.

(c) I wouldn't go into a witness box to defend it unless it had educational, artistic or psychiatric value to make it respectable.

(d) I read it only in the line of duty, and feel nothing but pity for those who read it for pleasure.

(e) Needless to say, I never masturbate.

Such—once you've stripped off the rhetoric—is the accepted liberal viewpoint; and safer than that you can hardly play. At best, it adds up to a vaguely progressive gesture that could never endanger the author's moral standing or give

11

his wife a moment's worry. From first to last he remains socially stainless and—to me, anyway—utterly unreal. He is like a man who loathes whorehouses in practice but doesn't mind defending them in principle, provided that they are designed by Mies van der Rohe and staffed by social workers in Balenciaga dresses.

At this point I had better offer a definition. By pornography I mean writing that is exclusively intended to cause sexual pleasure. I am not talking about novelists like D. H. Lawrence or Henry Miller; sex is often their theme, but titillation is never their main objective, and if they happen to arouse us, we keep ourselves resolutely zipped, aware that what we are feeling is only an incidental part of a large literary design. (This, of course, can be fairly frustrating at times. In *Lady Chatterley's Lover*, for instance, Lawrence has a teasing habit of getting the reader tumescent and suddenly changing the subject from sex to the dreadful side effects of the Industrial Revolution.) Nor am I concerned with the Anglo-Saxon exiles in Paris who used to concoct spare-time pornography under pseudonyms for the Olympia Press; straight smut wasn't their *métier*, and too often they strayed from the purpose at hand into irrelevant gags and other flights of asexual fancy. *Candy*, by Terry Southern and Mason Hoffenberg, is a brilliant example of pseudo-pornography, praised by the liberal critics precisely because it was too funny to be sexy. As the porter in *Macbeth* said of drink, 'It provokes the desire, but it takes away the performance.'

What we are discussing is something different—hard-core pornography, which is orgasmic in intent and untouched by the ulterior motives of traditional art. For men, it has a simple and localized purpose: to induce an erection. And the more skillfully the better. Contrary to popular myth, it takes discipline and devotion to be a first-rate pornographer, and only the subtlest command of rhythm and repetition will produce ideal results. These usually take the form of solo masturbation—usually, but not invariably, since vocal excerpts from bawdy books can often be employed to vary or intensify the customary fun of sexual coupling. In any case, the aim of pornography is physical enjoyment. Yet the liberals, at least, disdain it, and the public as a whole seems eager to burn it. I think it deserves a few words of exculpation and thanksgiving.

In 1962 John Osborne wrote a short and startling play called *Under Plain Cover*. It deals with a happily married suburban couple named Jenny and Tim, whose private life is entirely given up to the acting out of sexual fantasies. Sometimes she dresses up as a nurse, and he plays the apprehensive patient; in another version of the game he is a strict master threatening to punish a slovenly housemaid. They are both obsessed by Victorian knickers, of which they have a unique collection. After one fetishistic session, they meditate as follows:

JENNY: Do you think there are many people like us?
TIM: No. Probably none at all, I expect.
JENNY: Oh, there must be some.
TIM: Well, yes, but probably not two together.
JENNY: You mean just one on their own?
TIM: Yes.
JENNY: How awful. We are lucky.

Pornography is expressly designed for those who are not, in Jenny's sense, 'lucky'. If your taste is for earrings or high heels or spanking or any of the other minority appetites, you may have trouble finding a like-minded bedfellow. You will be 'one on their own', and that can create a strangulating sense of guilt. Pornography loosens the stranglehold and assuages the solitude; you know, at least, that you are not alone. Having bought a book that matches your fantasy, you emerge from the store with a spring-heeled stride and a surge of elation. I have felt that radiant contentment, and so have you—*hypocrite lecteur, mon semblable, mon-frère*. If chance denies you the right partner, that book and others like it will be your lifelong companions. Just as old habits die hard, old hards die habits.

The erotic minority man is not alone in needing the aid and comfort of pornography. Worse by far is the plight of those who are villainously ugly and unable to pay for the services of call girls. (If they are rich, their problem is negligible; beauty, after all, is in the eye of the stockholder.) To be poor and physically unappetizing is to be sexually condemned to solitary confinement, from which pornography offers the illusion of release. And we mustn't overlook its more commonplace uses. For men on long journeys, geographically cut off from wives and mistresses, pornography can act as a portable memory, a welcome shortcut to remembered bliss, relieving tension without involving disloyalty. And for uncommitted bachelors, arriving alone and short of cash in foreign cities where they don't speak the language, hard core is practically indispensable.

It's difficult to be an enemy of pornography without also disapproving of masturbation. In order to condemn the cause, it is logically necessary to deplore the effect. A century ago, when it was generally believed that self-stropping led to loss of hair, blindness and mental paralysis, I could have understood this attitude. Nowadays, I find it as baffling and repugnant as when I first encountered it, at the age of fourteen. The debating society at my school was discussing the motion 'That the present generation has lost the ability to entertain itself.' Rising to make my maiden speech, I said with shaky aplomb, 'Mr. Chairman—as long as masturbation exists, no one can seriously maintain that we have lost the ability to entertain ourselves.' The teacher in charge immediately closed the meeting. Today his successor would probably take a more tolerant view. But the old prohibitions still persist.

In a recent letter to the *Sunday Times*, a respected liberal clergyman wrote: 'To be sexually hungry is the fate of thousands, both young and old. There is nothing evil in this hunger, but it is hard to bear. To have it stimulated when it cannot be honourably satisfied is to make control more difficult.'

Here, in three short sentences, all the puritan assumptions are on parade— that sexual deprivation is the normal state of affairs, that it is morally desirable to grin and bear it, and that masturbation is a dishonourable alternative.

Because hard core performs an obvious physical function, literary critics have traditionally refused to consider it a form of art. By their standards, art is something that appeals to such intangibles as the soul and the imagination; anything that appeals to the genitals belongs in the category of massage. What they forget is that language can be used in many delicate and complex ways to enliven the penis. It isn't just a matter of bombarding the reader with four-letter words. As Lionel Trilling said in a memorably sane essay on the subject:

> I see no reason in morality (or in aesthetic theory) why literature should not have as one of its intentions the arousing of thoughts of lust. It is one of the effects, perhaps one of the functions, of literature to arouse desire, and I can discover no ground for saying that sexual pleasure should not be among the objects of desire which literature presents to us, along with heroism, virtue, peace, death, food, wisdom, God, etc.

That is the nutshell case for pornography as art. It could hardly be stated more concisely, and I have yet to hear it convincingly refuted. If a writer uses literary craft to provoke sexual delight, he is doing an artist's job. It is for him to decide whether four-letter words will help or hinder his design. C. S. Lewis, a great literary critic and Christian apologist, once jolted me by saying that he objected to venereal monosyllables mainly because they were anti-aphrodisiac; from antiquity onward, the best writers had found that the oblique approach to sex paid higher erotic dividends. ('The direct approach', he told me, 'means that you have to resort to the language of the nursery, the gutter or the medical textbook. And these may not be the associations you wish to evoke.') But that is a question of taste. Whatever technique the writer employs, we are entitled to judge the end product as a work of art. And the basic criterion, in the case of pornography, is whether or not it succeeds in exciting us. If it doesn't, we can write it off as an artistic failure.

Lawyers, as I discovered a couple of years ago, are not impressed by the Trilling doctrine. The English distributors of *Fanny Hill* were being prosecuted for obscenity, and the publishers' legal advisers asked me whether I would appear as a witness for the defence. I said I'd be delighted. And what form (they inquired) would my evidence take? I replied by pointing out that under English law obscenity is permissible as long as it has redeeming artistic merits. I considered erotic titillation a legitimate function of art, and therefore proposed to defend *Fanny Hill* on the ground that it was expertly titillating. The lawyers' professional smiles froze on their faces. They didn't exactly throw me out, but they made it arctically clear that I would not be called on to testify. In terms of courtroom tactics, they may have been right; it's just conceivable, however, that they missed a chance of establishing (or at least of testing) a new legal precedent. In any event, they lost the case.

But I mustn't lurch into the trap of suggesting that pornography is defensible only when it qualifies as art. It is defensible in its own right and for its own sake, no matter whether it is art or not, and whether it is well or badly written. Freedom to write about sex must include the freedom to write about it badly. Some of the younger critics—guerrillas at the gates of the literary Establishment—would go further and argue that pornography is not only different from art but in some respects more important. A reviewer in the *International Times*, London's underground newspaper, recently declared:

> In the brave new world of sexuality, perhaps we can forget about art, and read Henry Miller as he was meant to be read: as the writer whose craft describes intercourse better than anybody else's. If we have learned nothing else from Genet, we can be sure of this: his result may have been art, but that's not as important as his intention, which was pornography.

Very few critics, even today, can write about hard core without tremors of prejudice and preconception. You can sense them worrying all the time about what their readers will think of them; it mustn't be suspected that they enjoy it, because that would imply that they masturbate. So they get defensively jocose, or wearily condescending. They indulge in squirms of pity for those who actually go out and buy the stuff—the sort of pity that is twin brother of contempt. Of course, the hellfire preachers of popular reviewing don't bother with such petty qualms; for them, all pornography is subversive filth and ought to be destroyed unread. It's only in the work of intelligent critics that you hear the special tone of veiled liberal distaste, which is rather like that of a lecturer on toxicology who feels compelled to reassure us, every few seconds, that he has never actually poisoned anyone. This tone is audible, even in *The Other Victorians* by Steven Marcus, a much-praised and often perceptive study of pornography in nineteenth-century England. The author is an Associate Professor of English at Columbia. Let me list some of the errors, ambiguities and critical confusions that I detect in his book:

(1) Overdependence on Freudian dogma. Professor Marcus prefaces his text with the famous quotation in which Freud proclaims that 'the grandest cultural

achievements . . . are brought to birth by ever greater sublimation of the components of the sexual instinct'. In other words, the less energy you invest in sex, the more likely you are to produce a work of art. This is a hypothesis with no scientific basis of any kind. It is rather like saying that if you hoard enough milk, it may somehow turn into wine. The whole theory reeks of hidden puritanism, not to say magic.

(2) Overaddiction to Freudian symbolism. Describing a Victorian handbook on pornography, Professor Marcus points out that its author often hangs a page of footnotes on to a single line of text. He adds that 'one is tempted' to see in this 'an unconscious iconography: beneath a very small head there is attached a very large appendage'. Resist the temptation, Marcus: this is sub-Freudian tittering at its coyest. Later on, the professor quotes from a pornographer who casually—and to avoid repeating himself—uses the word 'evacuation' to mean ejaculation. 'If one expands the metaphor,' Marcus comments with pole-axing pedantry, 'one begins to see that the penis then might be either a fecal column or the lower end of the alimentary tract out of which fecal matter is to be expelled, the woman's body, particularly her genitals, becomes a toilet, etc.' Watch out for expanding metaphors, Marcus, especially if they're anal. Again, when a hard-core hero, busily undressing a girl, says that he 'unveiled beauties enough to bring the dead to life', the professor insists that the phrase is an unconscious reference to the author and his readers: *they* are the dead who need to be brought to life. If clichés can legitimately yield interpretations like that, we enter a minefield every time we uncover our typewriters.

(3) Verbal snobbery, i.e., the assumption that the sexual act is inherently too ignoble to be described in noble words. When a pornographer writes about 'that inner sovereignty or force, within my balls', Marcus gets witheringly scornful: 'An "inner sovereignty" that is yet "within my balls" is hopeless and impossible.

Sovereignty is toppled from its throne by being so located—there is nothing majestic about such an urgency.' This reminds me of a telling exchange at the Old Bailey in 1960, when *Lady Chatterley's Lover* was being tried for obscenity. Counsel for the prosecution, an Old Etonian and veteran of the Coldstream Guards, read a passage from the novel in tones of frigid derision and then asked Richard Hoggart, a young scholar giving evidence for the defence, whether he seriously contended that it was possible to feel 'reverence for a man's balls'. 'Indeed, yes,' said Hoggart, with quiet compassion for the fellow's obtuseness. He made it seem so obvious; and as he spoke you could feel the case swinging in Lawrence's favour.

(4) Facile generalization, based on sloppy research. This crops up in the brief, disdainful chapter that Marcus devotes to the vast Victorian literature of flagellation. In books of this genre, he says, 'what goes on is always the same. A person is accused of some wrongdoing. This person is most often a boy . . . The accuser is almost invariably some surrogate for his mother . . . An adult male figure, father or schoolmaster, occurs very infrequently.' In fact, the victim is usually a girl, and male accusers are just as common as female. The professor's reading list must have been curiously selective.

(5) Moral censure masquerading as stylistic disapproval. Marcus has a habit of attacking pornography in particular on grounds that apply to literature in general. At one point, for instance, he quotes a sentence that makes cloudy use of epithets such as 'voluptuous', 'amorous' and 'tumultuous'. He goes on to say that, because they are vague and unspecific, 'they express an important tendency in pornography'. Nothing of the sort: what they express is a tendency that exists in bad writing of any kind. Foggy prose is no more abhorrent in pornography than in Norman Vincent Peale.

But for all his lapses, Marcus is at least trying to be an objective witness, and often he succeeds. The roughest frontal assault on hard core in recent years has come from George Steiner, a sprightly American don who teaches at Churchill College, Cambridge. It was launched in an essay called 'Night Words', which Steiner contributed to the English magazine *Encounter*. He begins by contending that, since the number of sexual positions and combinations is limited, pornography is doomed to ultimate monotony. To which one replies that dawn and sunset are likewise limited, but that only a limited man would find them monotonous.

Already, quite early in the piece, there are signs that Steiner is easily bored. With a stoic yawn, he says that after any kind of sexual fulfilment 'there is the grey of morning and the sour knowledge that things have remained fairly generally the same since man first met goat and woman'. (Why grey instead of flesh-pink? Why sour rather than sweet? Why goats anyway?) Hereabouts he takes a sudden swerve that brings him into head-on collision with Professor Marcus, who is approaching from the opposite direction. According to Steiner, one of the definitions of abstract art is 'that it cannot be pornographic'. According to Marcus, pornography is 'in reality very abstract'.

Steiner now zeros in on his target. Reasonably enough, he maintains that there is no essential difference between 'erotic writing' and hard core except in the matter of verbal sophistication. But from this he argues that neither category 'adds anything new to the potential of human emotion; both add to the waste'. An assumption is buried here, and I trust you dig it: what Steiner means by waste is masturbation. A long passage follows in which he easily demolishes the pretensions of Maurice Girodias, founder of the Olympia Press, who is for ever protesting that what he published was not pornography but art. (My own complaint would be that although it was sometimes good art, it was always lousy pornography.) This section is dotted with words like 'bore', 'boredom', 'repetitive' and 'dull', just in case you are in any doubt about Steiner's attitude towards the desirability of writing about physical lovemaking. For what he is leading up to is nothing less than a blanket condemnation of all attempts to put the sexual act into words. He asserts that the best novelists leave sex in the wings; they stop at the bedroom door. To support his case he cites Tolstoy and George Eliot, both of whom lived at a time when it was forbidden to go further. As for modern outspokenness: 'There is no real freedom whatever in the compulsive physiological exactitudes of present "high pornography", because there is no respect for the reader whose imaginative means are set at nil.' Sex is a private citadel to be jealously guarded, an experience in which two human beings must find for themselves the mental images that will set their blood to racing in dark and wonder ever-renewed. (I am compressing, but not all that much.) 'The new pornographers', Steiner warns us dourly, 'subvert this last, vital privacy; they do our imagining for us.

They do our imagining for us. It sounds like a fearful affront, a chilling premonition of 1984; but in fact it is exactly what all good writers have done since the birth of literature. The measure of their talent has immemorially been their ability to make us see the world through their eyes. If they can heighten our perceptions, we should thank them, not resent them. And on the matter of privacy: I don't think Steiner is seriously suggesting that commando groups of scribbling voyeurs are going to burst into our bedrooms and take notes. We can always keep our sex lives to ourselves if we wish. But that doesn't mean (why should it?) that we must shrink from reading about other people's.

Steiner's climactic point is that hard core has no respect for 'the sanctity of autonomous life' as far as its characters are concerned. They don't exist in their own right, independent and self-sustaining, like people in Stendhal and Henry James. Pornographers, he says, 'shout at their personages: strip, fornicate, perform this or that act of sexual perversion.' The error here is one we have already noted in Marcus: Steiner is damning bad pornography for a crime that it shares with all bad fiction. Incompetent writers *always* shout at their characters: drink, take dope, perform this or that act of psychological perversion. In good pornography, as in good writing of any kind, the characters need no such external prompting. But Steiner goes on to compare pornographers with S.S. guards, who barked their orders at living men and women: 'The total attitudes are not, I think, entirely distinct. There may be deeper affinities than we as yet understand between the "total freedom" of the uncensored erotic imagination and the total freedom of the sadist. That these two freedoms have emerged in close historical proximity may not be coincidence.'

But have they? History refutes the argument. Sadists were indulging their grisly whims centuries before the modern era of sadistic pornography. Slaughter for fun is not a recent invention. Gilles de Rais was exploiting it to the full long before the Marquis de Sade began his missionary activities; like all enthusiasts of his kind, in whatever period, Gilles needed sadistic books to inflame him about as much as a Madras curry needs a pepper mill.

The question of banning de Sade has been urgently debated in England ever since the Moors Murder trial in 1966, at which a neofascistic Scot named Ian Brady and his mistress, Myra Hindley, were sentenced to life imprisonment for a series of explicitly sadistic killings. There victims were a seventeen-year-old youth and two children aged ten and twelve. Among the books found in Brady's lodgings was a study of the life and ideas of the Marquis de Sade. Did it supply him with fantasy scenarios which he later enacted in reality? Was this a case of life imitating art? Pamela Hansford Johnson, the novelist and wife of C. P. Snow, suspects that it might have been, and has poured her qualms into an agitated little book called *On Iniquity*. In it she comes out strongly against the free dissemination of pornography. 'There is a tyranny of libertarianism as well as of restriction,' she says, 'and we can already hear its baying, and the rolling of its tumbrils.' Miss Hansford Johnson is no professional bigot; she is a decent liberal in a state of sincere unease; but a cool survey of the facts suggests that her natural horror at the Brady-Hindley crimes has carried her to irrational extremes. Brady's record shows that he was cutting up live cats with a flick knife at the age of ten; and around the same time he tied up a school friend and tried to burn him to death. He was a practising sadist before he ever heard of de Sade.

To my mind, the really evil books about physical cruelty are those which give it a moral justification. I am thinking, for example, of those Catholic tracts that appeared at the bloody high noon of the Inquisition, telling true believers that it was necessary to maim and incinerate unrepentant heretics for the good of their souls. I think, too, of military manuals on the use of bayonets and small arms, which teach you how to inflict the most refined and crippling pain for the greater good of your country. I despise such books and regret that there are people who like to read them. But I would not ban them.

One inalienable right binds all mankind together—the right of self-abuse. That—and not the abuse of others—is what distinguishes the true lover of pornography. We should encourage him to seek his literary pleasure as and where he finds it. To deny him that privilege is to invade the deepest privacy of all.

A PANDORA'S BOX OF DEFINITIONS

ENTER A PORNO MOVIE theatre these days and you sense an intensity of personal concentration any performer or teacher would envy. Unless the theatre is over-crowded, each spectator observes the territorial imperative of separating himself from his neighbor as far as available seating will permit. Apart from an occasional defensive laugh or remark—obviously from a tourist —the sound of sporadic sno-ring from those who have come to escape the street, or the snap of a beer can tab, the atmosphere is hushed, almost reverential. Each spectator-communicant directs towards the flickering images on the screen a distilled intensity born of his innermost, ultimately unsharable, needs. The photography may be poor, the sound track undecipherable, the narrative nonexistent, but the sexual images have the power to mesmerize because they connect powerfully with the devotee's need to fantasize.

This silent, almost religious concentration contrasts sharply with the atmosphere of the stag "smoker" of yesteryear. Before the public surfacing of pornography, viewing a dirty movie was for generations of American males an activity charged with the dual tensions of illegality and personal anxiety. The men who gathered regularly in the American Legion meeting hall or fraternity house club room had to prove to their fellows that they were worthy of participating in the stag ritual. Their sexual ignorance was masked, their private needs socialized through the forced bravado of laughter and collective sexual banter. The raucous display of verbal *machismo* avoided the embarrassment of individual confrontation with sexual images that were all the more potent because they were forbidden.

A Free Ride, 1915.

25

The stag film or dirty movie was, and is, the *cinéma vérité* of the forbidden, an invaluable record of the images openly unacknowledged feelings about sex assume. In a time when verbal and visual images of sex were suppressed, when open art could only euphemize, the stags documented those isolated and unmentionable private experiences which were nonetheless in some form universal. By sharing the mysteries of sexual data through collective rituals of masculine emergence, American and European males (primarily the former) received through the stags a non-credit course in sex education. The films proved that a world of sexuality existed outside one's limited individual experiences. Here were real people and real sexual activity made all the more real because their esthetic embodiment was so weak, the "performers" so clearly not "actors."

The stag film encapsulates fantasies and creates them, for if art imitates life, life also imitates art—even (some might say particularly) bad art. That most stags have been crude, esthetically dismissable is true; the form was rigid, the economics difficult, the penalties often stringent, and, of course, the values almost exclusively male, hence the designation "stag."

This emphasis has caused some feminists to attack pornography as an instrument in the degradation and subjugation of women. Although this is not the place for a detailed consideration of this objection, one brief observation is appropriate. Since sado-masochism plays a very small part in the traditional stag film (see the later section on its Themes and Variations), if women are "degraded" as sex objects in these films, it is rarely because they are actively humiliated, but rather because they engage in sex without their larger reality as individuals being acknowledged. But in this regard their male partners are treated no differently; indeed, they are even less "humanized" than the women, who are, after all, the focus of attention. Occasionally these men are grotesquely masked, even sexually inept. They exist only as surrogates for the male audience. They are

"What a beautiful dairy."
A Free Ride, 1915.

26

the means whereby the individual fantasist possesses his lust's desire, an image idealized as often as it is demeaned. To say that both men and women are degraded equally because of the specialization of their performance seems as sensible as claiming that clowns, acrobats, or ball players are degraded because as performers they are not visible in their full humanity.

A Free Ride, 1915.

Two French Wildcats, 1930's.

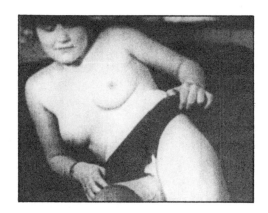

Author's True Story, 1932-1936.

Pornography is a theatre of types—a limited genre in which specialized skills and subject matter are explored to the exclusion of others. As Susan Sontag has pointed out: "It is the nature of the pornographic imagination to prefer ready-made conventions of character, setting, and action." Lust is the emotion which determines its esthetic. In such an enclosed universe—one which most of us have at various times entered—it is axiomatic that the complete social and psychological individual—male or female—is unwelcome. In the absence of compulsion, there is no commanding reason why those men and women who depict lust, who arouse it in us, must inevitably degrade or be degraded.

Pornographic films—stag and porno—indeed involve male fantasies of sexual activity divorced from social and psychological complications. But these fantasies are not inconsequential; they map an inner psychic landscape no less vivid than documentary reality. For this reason, discussions of pornography and pornographic films are misdirected. It is often claimed that the dependence upon fantasy robs pornography of serious import. "Nothing as negative as real life is permitted to intrude," write Arthur Knight and Hollis Alpert in their *Playboy* history of the stag film, "if the producer of pornography can help it." Accepting the distinction drawn by Eberhard and Phyllis Kronhausen in *Pornography and the Law*, Knight and Alpert distinguish the "erotic realism" of art from the supersexual evasions of pornographic fantasy. The frequency with which this distinction appears in writing on pornography reveals a parochial isolation from the forms this esthetic dualism has generally assumed in art and literary criticism. (The oppositions between realism and romance or naturalism and expressionism are but two instances.)

Indeed, the realism-fantasy antithesis is at the heart of film esthetics. At the risk of oversimplification, one might broadly divide film theories into those which stress the film's capacity to document, to record, to celebrate the physical world, and those which affirm the film's potential to create fantasies or visions (either rooted in reality or esthetically autonomous). Film, writes one critic, is "by definition an act of illusion." And this illusion of motion created by the persistence of vision has the unique capacity to evoke through editing the perception of the dream or the daydream. From its origins film both recorded and transmuted reality in the documentary travelogues of Lumière and the visions of the illusionist Méliès. The dual goals are not irreconcilable. As Jean-Luc Godard paradoxically noted in *La Chinoise*, from one vantage point Lumière is an "illusionist" in that he relies upon the esthetic conventions of impressionism; and Méliès, despite his artifice, in transforming the infant cinema into a kind of Brechtian newsreel, affirmed a modern, "realistic" sensibility.

To equate realism with art and fantasy with non-art is, then, simplistic. In fiction, theatre, or film documentary realism, often called naturalism—the faithful description of the surface of reality—is an esthetic method no older than the history of film itself, and is dependent upon the deepest kind of illusionism: it asks us to willingly suspend our conscious knowledge of the artificial conventions that contrive its "reality." Clearly all art—and particularly film, with its ability to capture the fleeting image—has the capacity to depict both observed and conjured worlds, worlds which invariably interpenetrate.

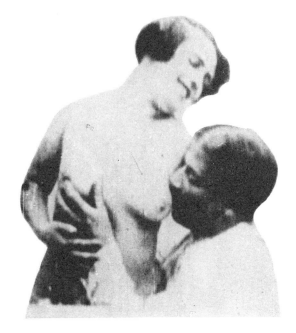

The Chiropodist, 1922-1927.

WE HAVE EMBARKED on treacherous terrain. Obscenity, pornography, erotica: the terms are sometimes used synonymously, sometimes differently. "To define pornography or obscenity precisely," writes Alma Birk, chairperson of the British Health Education Council, "has proved beyond the wit of man. Maybe we should stop trying." But we persist. The current feminist debate has produced a new proliferation of theoretical broadsides to take their places on the shelves beside *Does Pornography Matter?*, *The Esthetics of Pornography*, *Art and Pornog-*

Strictly Union, 1919.

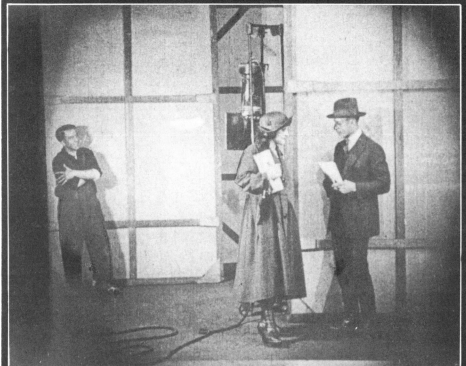

"The day starts at the Fuckem Right Studios."

"Hard Penis. The property boy, who is a strictly union worker."

"A stiff prick has no conscience."

" So you're going to be a bathing gal, hey."   "No, no. Don't do that."

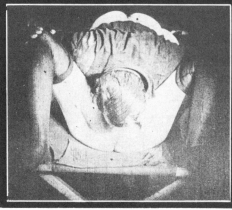

"Minnie Womb. An extra with ambition and a great future in front of her."

raphy, etc. Indeed, the literature on pornography has far exceeded (until the recent commercial flood) the literature *of* pornography. If Justice William J. Brennan was right when he said, "I know it when I see it," one wonders why it has been so difficult for our culture to describe what it sees.

Even the prophets of sexual liberation—themselves little more than a decade released from the pillory of the obscene—are no help. D. H. Lawrence, in his attack on "sex in the head," castigates pornography as the unpardonable "attempt to insult sex, to do dirt on it." Henry Miller similarly reviles pornography "as the round-about, leering or lecherous disguise which only adds to the murk." Obscenity, on the other hand, is cleansing, he continues, "because whenever a taboo is broken, something vitalizing happens, another step towards greater truth and honesty and openness." But not infrequently, particularly in the law, obscenity and pornography are used interchangeably, even though most would agree that semantically obscenity is the broader category since it subsumes the scatological as well as the sexual and includes actions as well as words and images.

The term "obscenity" serves as the vehicle of our deepest disgust. Although it can be meaningful in socially agreed-upon circumstances, at present disgust is aroused so variously the word is robbed of any but expressive meaning. For many it is used as a synonym for the gross, the grotesque, the hateful ("The Vietnam War is obscene!"); for others it still connotes the coarse, taboo vernacular of sex and excretion. In short, apart from the law, where it is often most obscure where it should be most precise, it is a word that now functions metaphorically. In accordance with its presumed etymology, it represents any word, artifact, or action so loathsome as to be consciously thrust from view, *ob scena*—off stage.

"Pornography" is used in a more limited sense as an esthetic construct rather than as a characteristic of language or behavior. However defined, it can be viewed from different perspectives. Sontag has observed that there are at least

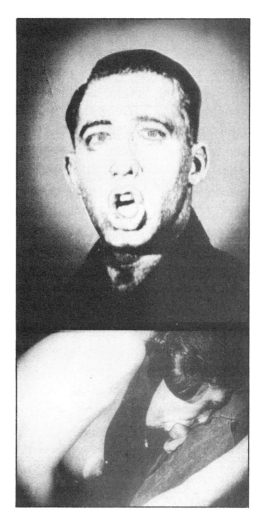

"**All right then,** come on downtown for lunch."
Strictly Union, 1919.

31

The Chiropodist, 1922-1927.

three pornographies (i.e., three modes of its analysis) which must be considered individually: pornography as an item in social history, pornography as a psychological phenomenon, and pornography as "a minor but interesting modality or convention within the arts." To these one might add a fourth, that which delimits the others: pornography (obscenity) as a criminal action in the eyes of the law. However approached, the concept of pornography is particularly elusive because it has functioned often simultaneously within moral, legal, and esthetic categories. The debate as to whether or not pornography is or can be art rests, then, on this distinction: if pornography is defined descriptively as a distinct genre with established conventions, there is no reason why it cannot, like any sub-genre, be raised to "art" by a writer, painter, or film maker of talent; if pornography is judged to be a form which demands a simplistic distortion of human behavior and values, it may well be excluded by definition.

The situation is further obscured by the fact that pornography is a relatively recent term used to encompass a previous body of historical material. The first recorded usage of the word in English (see the *Oxford English Dictionary*) is in 1850, though the word undoubtedly emerged earlier. Despite its Greek etymology (literally, writings by or about prostitutes), there is almost no classical reference to "pornography." The German scholar Licht found the word *pornographos*—a writer about whores—only once in his reading of classical literature. The term must orginate in the attempt to designate the category of erotic writing initiated by Aretino in the sixteenth century. His *Ragionamenti*, or *Discussions*, consciously assumes the form of the Greek writer Lucian's *Dialogues of the Whores*, which is less an erotic work than a collection of anecdotes showing that whores were a socially exploited class that had to work at survival. Aretino's work consists of a series of dialogues in which a successful courtesan recounts her sexual adventures in the course of offering her daughter advice about the choices open

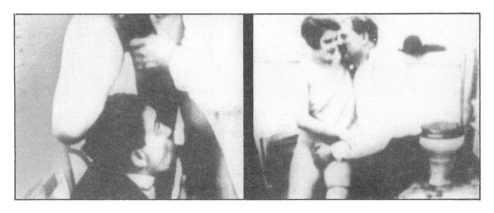

"Tit for tat you suck the prick and I suck that tit." *The Chiropodist*, 1922-1927.

to women. With the emergence of other works about prostitutes such as *The Whore's Rhetoric*, *La Puttana Errante*, and *Memoirs of a Woman of Pleasure* in the seventeenth and eighteenth centuries, the original designation *pornography* was literally correct.

As with all living esthetic categories, the evolution of form burst the constrictions of literal definition. From Chorier's *Satyra Sotadica* (1660)—the first obsessional sexual work—a distinctive literary form evolved, a form single-mindedly dedicated to the description of sexuality unlimited by the world of procurement. By the heyday of sexual prudery in the Victorian era, erotic fiction had ripened into a mature literary genre with individual sub-variants. It was, of course, a form progressively defined by its growing illegality. As overt descriptions and depictions of sexuality, regardless of esthetic merit, were proscribed in open literature and art, their collective energies, diverted underground, swelled the pornographic tide.

The Magician, 1930's.

33

Matinee Idol, 1930's.

To apply the term pornographic, then, to any overt sexual image or description, to lump together such diverse phenomena as Indian temple sculpture, Japanese "shunga" (erotic prints), Rowlandsonian bawdiness, Aristophanic phallicism, and Chaucerian scatology, is to confuse subject matter with the means of its expression. Even the term "erotica" is misleading in this context, for although it attempts to avoid the value-laden connotations of pornography or obscenity, it appears to describe a specific body of esthetically coherent material, rather than a diverse assortment of genres and styles with the common subject matter of sexuality.

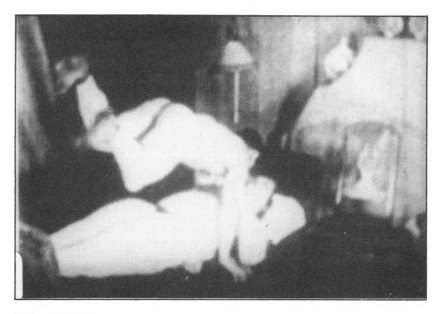

Matinee Idol, 1930's.

THE RISE OF PORNOGRAPHY

ALTHOUGH ITS FANTASIES, impulses, and imagery are trans-historical, pornography is a specific historical phenomenon. And, although the proscription of certain actions, ideas, and representations is virtually universal, the crime of obscenity—the legal condemnation of sexual imagery—is scarcely two centuries old. Historically, most Western societies have been more concerned with sedition and blasphemy than with obscenity. It was not until the eighteenth century that common, as opposed to ecclesiastical, law was applied to obscene libel in England, and not until the nineteenth century that specific legislation authorized the prosecution of obscene materials. Pornography and censorship have coexisted symbiotically, the greater the suppression, the faster the rise.

Pornography heralds the increasing hostility of the artist towards society. By the seventeenth century sexual license is linked with explicit attacks on religious and social conventions; in the eighteenth century erotic writing details sexual orgies in religious and pseudo-religious orders and attacks the institution of the family through the incest theme. This rebellious trend is definitively expressed in the anarchism of De Sade. The marquis articulates what lies behind pornography's obsessional detail: the superiority of the senses to established moral codes, a Hobbesian naturalism which sees aggression

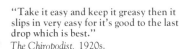

"Take it easy and keep it greasy then it slips in very easy for it's good to the last drop which is best."
The Chiropodist, 1920s.

35

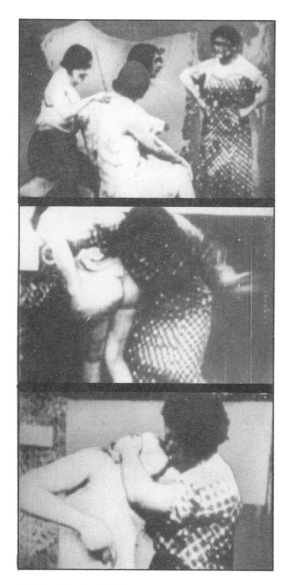

beneath the veneer of social forms, and the assumption that society is based on hypocrisy, that those who do not acknowledge sexuality's claims are fools or liars.

Perhaps the first book to be almost totally preoccupied with sexuality is Nicholas Chorier's *Satyra Sotadica*, published in 1660, about the time that the prose novel emerged in Europe. It claimed to be the work of a Spanish court lady named Luisa Sigea and consists of dialogues about sex among girls with Latin names. It repeatedly harks back to classical times as a sexual golden age far superior to the degenerate present. However, Chorier's work, although based on that of Aretino and Lucian before him, is in sensibility quite different; it obsessively catalogues a range of sexual variations, following the principle of erotic intensification found in later pornography—progressing from simple coupling and lesbianism through buggery to orgies, incest, flagellation, and other forms of

The French Teacher, 1920's.

sado-masochism. And all these activities take place within a tightly knit family. As Wayland Young has remarked: "It is the first work of rigid specialization, and thousands of later works have done no more than ring the changes on it."

The first English work in the pornographic mainstream, still probably the hardiest, is not nearly as obsessive—John Cleland's *Memoirs of a Woman of Pleasure*, first published in two volumes in 1748-49. Written in the epistolary mode of the early English novel, *Fanny Hill*, as Cleland's *Memoirs* came to be known after its irrepressible heroine, is almost a counter-statement to Richardson's *Clarissa*. The latter reeks with a sexuality never spoken. Clarissa's seduction, or rape, by Lovelace, although the hinge upon which the novel turns, occurs mysteriously, almost invisibly. *Fanny Hill*, on the other hand, although it provides the reader with some social background, truncates narrative and psychological detail to concentrate on the sexual experiences of its heroine, who, unlike Clarissa, is not destroyed by her sexual adventures.

The persecuted maiden fares far worse, of course, in the work of the Marquis de Sade, who defined a tradition distinct from, yet a part of, the mainstream of literary pornography. Together with the detailed descriptions of extreme sexual

"Don't you think that is a Daisy?"
The Casting Couch, 1924.

Film title unknown.

An English Tragedy, 1920-1926.

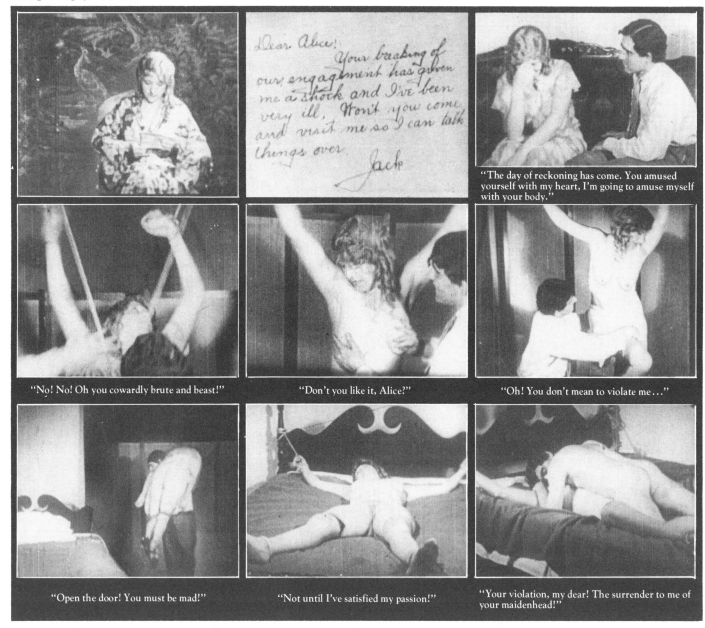

activities which reflected De Sade's proclivities—those "honored" with the designation of his name—there are the instincts of a moralist and serious artist. His work is intended not only as a means of controlling his fantasies by depicting them, but as a reverse image of the complacent values of his culture. De Sade is the clearest, most powerful example of the pornographer as transgressor. The first great transvaluer of values, he took piety, conformity, even pleasure itself, and inverted them. With its passionate personal hatred of God and Virtue, his writing offered the first detailed blueprint of the unspeakable depths beneath the facade of human rationality.

Most pornography does not display the parochial intensity of De Sade's monomania, despite the presence of various sado-masochistic practices in many mainstream works. Flagellation, for example—which had been morally legitimized by religious and pedagogical practice—so characterized British pornography as to become known as *le vice anglais*; it is particularly omnipresent in Victorian pornography, with the man as often the subject of physical abuse (the governess, nanny syndrome) as the woman (the servant syndrome).

Indeed, when we think of pornography today we tend to accept the conventions of the form established in its late Victorian heyday. Steven Marcus has coined the word "pornotopia" to describe the universe that emerges from Victorian pornographic fiction; pornography, he observes, despite its apparent designation of a physical setting, actually takes place nowhere, that is, in a world where environmental detail is irrelevant, where the *lingua franca* of sex is the national language. Time is irrelevant as well: "What time is it in pornotopia?" "It is always bedtime." Life begins not with birth, but with one's initial sexual impulse or experience. And nature is celebrated, in florid detail, only in the presence of the supine female form whose moist "cavern" is the center of the universe and the home of man. As in utopia, the impediments of mundane reality do not exist:

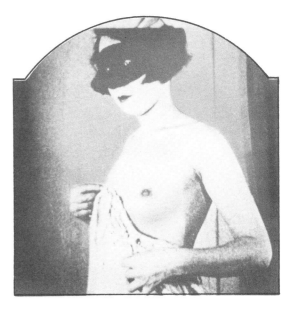

Wonders of the Unseen World, 1927.

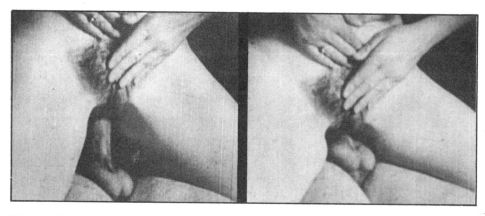

Wonders of the Unseen World, 1927.

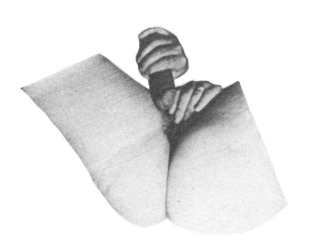

Wonders of the Unseen World, 1927.

men are forever potent; women are always in heat; both are sexually inexhausti-ble as well as infinitely pliable in their sexual gymnastics.

This paradigm of pornographic values does not hold universally, however. Neither *Fanny Hill, Justine, Dolly Morton, Grushenka, Lust,* nor *The Enormous Bed* (to name a few), is devoid of temporal or historical specificity. But it does characterize much of the genre, particularly its more obsessive examples. One thing is clear—pornotopia is a literary construct; it is difficult to create visually because pictorial art, particularly film, demands a concrete (even if imagined) reality. Since film, like fiction, exists in time, the stag film as it emerged absorbed the conventions of literary pornography in much the same way that public movies fed on existing literary and theatrical themes and forms. But since the stag was a particularly brief form, it had neither world enough nor time to exploit narrative conventions, though the early stag, as we shall see, makes a stronger attempt to do so than its successors.

ENTER THE STAG

STAG, PORNOGRAPHIC, BLUE, DIRTY MOVIE: the terms are synonymous. American usage has preferred "stag," the British "blue." The films illustrated in this book comprise a generous selection of the genre we shall refer to as the stag film, that is, the (usually) illegal filmic depiction of actual, non-simulated sexual acts, produced for private viewing or for showing in officially decried but socially tolerated circumstances (the brothel, the "smoker"). Those films which have been shown publicly in the United States since 1970 we refer to as "pornos." They represent both a continuation of and a divergence from the stag genre.

The development of new technology in the nineteenth century led to its appropriation for pornographic purposes. Images of sexuality in drawing, painting, printing, and sculpture had, of course, antedated the invention of photographic processes, but these were artists' visions and recreations of reality rather than depictions of reality itself. As photography transformed our esthetic perception of the world, pornography could not long remain unaffected. Within a few years of the introduction of the daguerrotype process in 1839, portrait studios opened all over the world, and by 1853 the New York *Tribune* estimated that at least 3 million daguerrotypes were taken annually in the United States alone. It did not estimate, however, the percentage of those that might have been pornographic. That the daguerrotype was soon used for erotic purposes is proven by the presence in the archives of the Institute for Sex Research (the ISR) at Indiana University of pornographic daguerrotypes that date back as far as the 1840s.

The Casting Couch, 1924.

41

The Casting Couch, 1924.

The daguerrotype had severe technical limitations; it demanded long exposures which were made directly onto a sensitized copper plate. Since no negative was involved in the process, each daguerrotype was and is a unique original and thus unreproducible. With the development of wet- and dry-plate processes, exposure time was not only radically reduced, but multiple prints were possible from an original negative. These developments greatly aided the pornographic exploitation of photography—the peddling of "feelthy peectures" proliferated. Fernand Drujon's *Catalogue of Suppressed and Condemned Works* in 1879 listed sixty-eight individuals convicted for selling *photographies obscènes ou prohibés*. The evidence clearly reveals that photos of explicit sexual activity are about as old as photography itself.

It follows that when motion pictures were developed in the 1890s the erotic possibilities were not long unexplored. Although it is impossible to determine exactly when the first stag film was produced, sexual titillation is present in film from its very beginnings. Lo Duca, in *L'Erotisme au Cinema II*, includes stills from an 1896 film, *Le Bain*, in which an actress, Louise Willy, disrobes completely. Many early French film catalogues list similar attempts at "cheesecake." In Germany a producer named Oskar Messter offered such fare as girls disrobing, exercising, dancing, or bathing. In America the *Kiss* series (featuring a May Irwin-John Rice kiss and the "Bowery Kiss" of Kid Foley and Sailor Lil) were offered to peep- and road-show audiences as pictorial representations of "leading exponents of the art of artistical embraces."

This material, although increasingly censured officially, was openly and publicly shown. The first clandestine erotic film remains unknown. Lo Duca dates one film, *Le Voyeur*, as early as 1907. Ado Kyrou's filmography of scenarios of *"un certain cinéma clandestin"* in the film journal *Positif* offers a full description of a film called *A l'Ecu d'Or ou la Bonne Auberge* ("At the Golden Shield or the

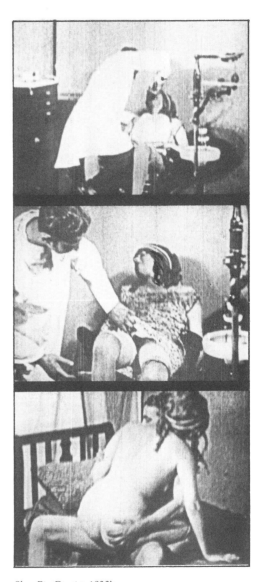

Slow-Fire Dentist, 1920's.

43

The Pick Up, 1923.

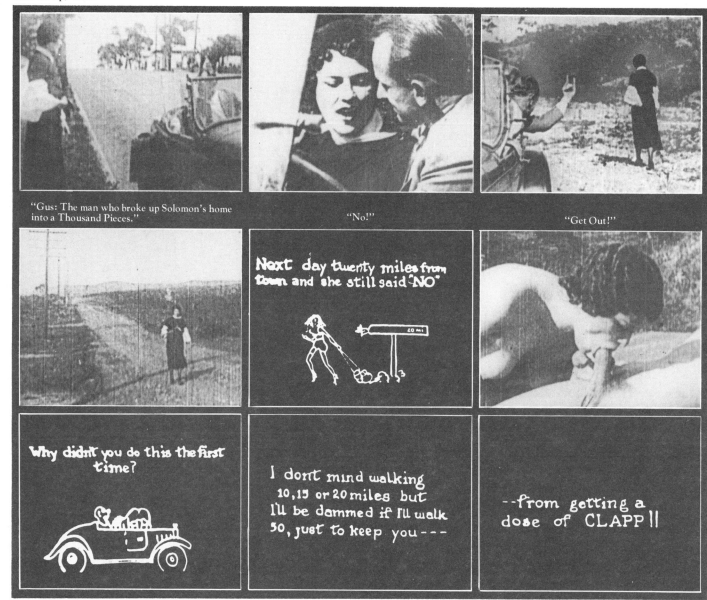

"Gus: The man who broke up Solomon's home into a Thousand Pieces."

"No!"

"Get Out!"

Next day twenty miles from town and she still said "NO"

Why didn't you do this the first time?

I dont mind walking 10,15 or 20 miles but I'll be dammed if I'll walk 50, just to keep you---

--from getting a dose of CLAPP !!

44

Good Inn"), definitively dated 1908. Kyrou describes it as "the oldest pornographic film having a scenario." His summary of the one-reeler follows: "During wartime, a valiant musketeer presents himself famished at the door of an inn. 'Nothing left to eat,' answers the innkeeper. Happily, thanks to an accommodating servant girl, an *amorous* meal is offered him. He enjoys it so much that, on the appearance of another girl, he demands a second helping."

Although the evidence is sparse, it indicates that the pioneer stag film makers, working during the first decade of the twentieth century, were French. This accords with the general pattern of film history, for Louis Lumière's inventive and marketing genius had put France in the lead as a film producer and exporter for more than a decade. The Edison *kinetoscope*—launched with explosive but shortlived success in 1894—was an unwieldy, immovable monster;

The Pick Up, 1923.

45

The Casting Couch, 1924.

Lumière's 1895 *cinématographe,* on the other hand, weighed only five kilograms, about a hundredth of the Edison camera. Handcranked, independent of electricity, it was the ideal instrument for catching life on the run, *sur le vif,* as Lumière put it. Erotic life did not long remain undocumented.

Alpert and Knight, in their *Playboy* study of the stag film, claim that there is evidence that a market for pornographic films existed as early as 1904, with Buenos Aires as a principal center of production: "Movies of fully detailed sexual activity were shot and shipped to private buyers, mostly in England and France, but also in such distant lands as Russia and the Balkan countries." The purchasers of the films were either rich aristocrats or houses of prostitution. "By the end of *la belle époque,*" they continue, "no self-respecting brothel in any of the large cities on the Continent considered its facilities complete without a stock of these films." If by *la belle époque* Alpert and Knight mean the period ended by the outbreak of the Great War rather than the turn of the century, the broadness of their claim may well be correct. Since brothels have traditionally presented erotic "entertainments" of various kinds to stimulate recalcitrant energies (eighteenth and nineteenth century brothels often staged elaborate erotic spectacles), it is logical that such films must have been presented as soon as technologically feasible. Indeed, before the Second World War in France and other countries the showing of pornographic films in brothels was customary and officially permitted.

As for Buenos Aires as a production center, we know that stags were customarily shown in its red-light districts. They seem, however, on the evidence of Louis Sheaffer's biography of Eugene O'Neill, to have been imported from France or Spain rather than locally produced. The stags made a great impression on the young O'Neill; in his *Bound East for Cardiff* (1916), the dying Yank reminisces with his buddy Driscoll about the raucous past: "D'yuh remember the times we had in Buenos Aires? The moving pictures in Barracas? Some class to them, d'yuh remember?" Later in life, O'Neill further described the "class" of the films he had witnessed as a seaman in Barracas, a suburb of Buenos Aires, in 1910-11: "Those pictures were mighty rough stuff. Nothing was left to the imagination. Every form of perversity was enacted and, of course, the sailors flocked to them."

In the United States we can deduce that explicitly sexual films must have been made before the oldest extant film in the ISR archive, *A Free Ride* (also known as *A Grass Sandwich*), dated about 1915, because its technique was already quite developed for the genre. We speak, of course, in highly relative terms, for until recently the history of the stag film has been one of arrested esthetic development. For most of its history it has remained fixed in the formal mold of the film in its infancy, and in that restrictive one-reel form it survives today in the very milieu in which the American film first emerged—the peep show. The general public has always been suspicious of the darkened, potentially dangerous, partitioned areas of the penny arcade, and it was not until the movies ventured out of the tenderloin onto the open road, to street fairs, picnics, benefits, church socials, and medicine shows, that they were firmly established in America as a widely popular medium. As they moved further into the theatres and vaudeville houses, ambitious entrepreneurs rushed in to meet the rising demand for projectable material.

Until the success of D. W. Griffith's *Enoch Arden* in 1911 established for the first time in America the two-reel film as a formal unit, the infant cinema compressed reality and fiction into the confines of the single reel, although the length of this reel increased steadily. The subjects of the early one-reelers were universal: sports events; documentary panoramas of seasides, waterfalls, winter scenes, trains, etc.; vaudeville acts—acrobats, jugglers, dancers, magicians; and improvised incidents and short skits which embodied the popular ideas, aspira-

Slow-Fire Dentist, 1920's.

tions, and issues of the day. These early comedy-adventures established a simple, naive form which served as the basis for the emerging American stag film. The central figure in these comedies was invariably a common man or woman—farmer, fireman, policeman, housewife, stenographer, clerk, servant, rube, spinster—with whom an unsophisticated audience could identify. Within the limitations of the single reel there was usually only time for the presentation of one comic incident. Such is the case in the classic American stag—the hero is more often plebian than upper class, and the structure of the film is based upon a single action, now sexual.

The early public one-reelers (1903-08) often sneaked erotic "teasers" into the action: *Making Love in a Hammock, Love in a Broker's Office*, and *Lovers Interrupted* were humorous skits of illicit lovemaking with the hammock collapsing or the wife arriving *before* the climactic moment was achieved. Other comedies burlesqued the trials and tribulations of domestic life: *Gaities of Divorce, If*

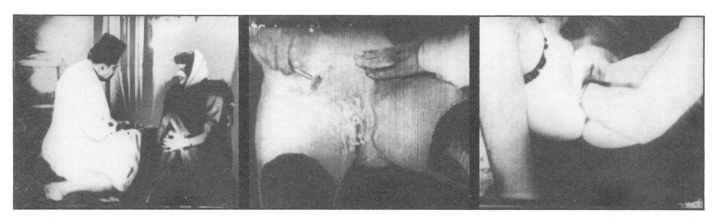

Bare Interlude, 1928-1933.

You Had a Wife Like This, and *Married Again.* Others, like *Old Man's Darling, A Seaside Flirtation, Beware My Husband Comes, College Boy's First Love, Love at Each Floor,* and *Parisienne's Bedtime*, were more provocatively titled. Many of these are would-be stag films, and it is easy to see how one could retard the mate's discovery or the hammock's collapse. Since the early days of film production were anarchic, the pioneer film makers were less restricted than those who worked in established forms. As the film grew in popularity and commercial viability, however, the forces of censorship, alarmed at such films as those above and crime films as well, exerted increased control. By 1907-08 the movies began to hew a tighter moral line. Sentimentality grew and erotic teasers drastically diminished. As the early film became more respectable it increasingly embodied established—often pernicious—moral and social values. Witness, for example, *The Masher,* a film which shows a lady-killer rebuffed by all the girls with whom he flirts. Finally, he is successful, only to discover that his conquest is a black

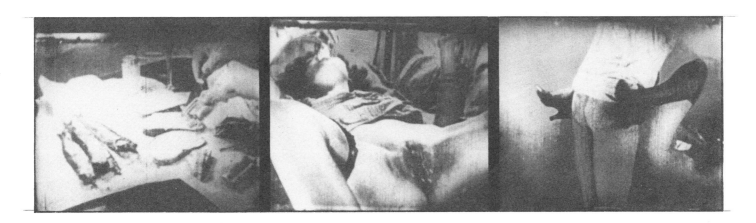

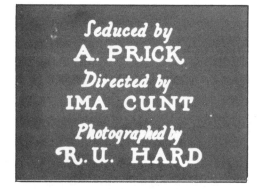

Wonders of the Unseen World, 1927.

woman, whereupon he runs for dear life (regretfully, a "bit" Buster Keaton resurrected in *Seven Chances*). Although the stag film is not without its evidences of racism, no masher *ever* runs from such encounters. If there is one vice the stag film universally deplores it is hypocrisy.

A Free Ride—the earliest extant American stag film—is filmicly almost indistinguishable from its slightly older, one-reel public contemporaries. With its outdoor milieu, its many and varied set-ups, its heavy use of titles, its concentration on the rhythms of a single incident, its obvious professionalism in technique, and its ordinary plot mechanism (a car ride), it derives from the same sources as the open films of the first decade, with one essential difference—the explicitness of its depiction of sexual activity. The plot is simple: a man picks up two girls and takes them for a drive in the country. He stops the car in a wooded area, gets out,

Two French Wildcats, 1930's.

and walks behind a bush to relieve himself. The girls, curious, spy on him, become excited, and have to urinate themselves. The tables are turned. The man spies on them and, emboldened by lust, initiates unopposed sexual contact with one of the girls; her friend watches and before long demands her share of his attention. Soon "all's well that ends well" and the "free ride" is over. As Professor Frank Hoffmann has pointed out, the film displays all the basic characteristics of the stag film genre: sexual excitment of the female and male by visual means, a direct and rapid seduction (so rapid as hardly to constitute a seduction at all), and sexual activity as the primary focus of the film. A *Free Ride* is also particularly American in its early association of the automobile and sex, a theme evident in such later films as *The Pick Up* (1920s and 1950s versions), *A Highway Romance*, *Pick Ups*, and *A Modern Hitchhiker* (all the latter from the 1930s).

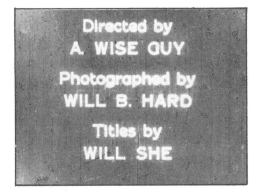

A Free Ride, 1915.

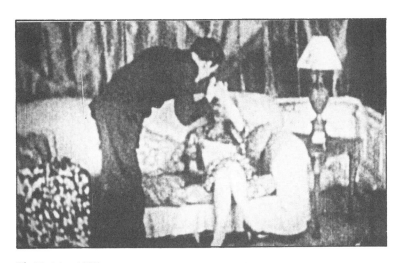

The Magician, 1930's.

Strictly Union, 1919.

"WONDERS OF THE UNSEEN WORLD"

SOCIAL, LEGAL, AND COMMERCIAL forces combined to fix the form of the stag film at the point achieved in its infancy in *A l'Ecu d'Or* and *A Free Ride*. For over half a century it remained essentially a severely limited, remarkably consistent genre, despite variations of decade and national taste. Indeed, the illegal, unregulated nature of its commerce meant that the same films, duplicated and reduplicated, surfaced at different times and places, often under different main titles. And, since it was a silent form, linguistic barriers were not significant (translated inter-titles could be spliced into the print of a foreign film when necessary). Yet there was far less interchange of films than one might expect. A limited amount of international material emerged on the American market. Although the evidence suggests that the principal producers of stag films were France, Germany, Italy, the United States, Latin America, and Japan, only French and Mexican films appeared in any numbers in the United States. Despite myths of giant vice overlords and profiteers, the production of pornographic films has been an haphazard, high-risk, low-profit, regional activity. Films were, for the most part, produced in series in regional centers and initially distributed in their immediate areas. The stag film was, in essence, a cottage industry, and despite the pirating of duplicate prints, most films available in a country, or even in one part of a country, apparently were produced in that country or region.

For these reasons and, of course, given the underground, illegal nature of the entire enterprise, it is impossible to estimate accurately the number of different stag films made from 1915 to 1970, or the number of surviving prints. Alpert and Knight estimate that even two thousand titles might be too small a number. On the basis of about four hundred reels of film he analyzed at the ISR—largely American materials—Professor Hoffmann notes that before the 1950s there appear to have been two peaks of stag production: the mid-1920s—the period of the development of sixteen-millimeter film—and the few years prior to World War II. Kyrou, in his *Positif* filmography, cites the years 1930 to 1938 as *l'âge d'or du*

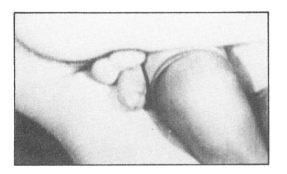

Hot Party, 1928-1933.

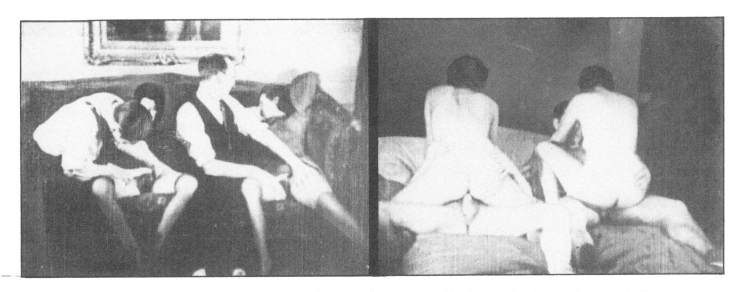

"Two girls who are fugitives from the grand hotel decide that strange interlude at their apartment is like a lot of laughter in hell with a silver dollar."
Hot Party, 1928-1933.

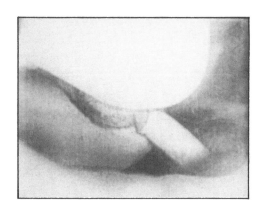

Matinee Idol, 1930's.

film erotique; more than forty films a year were produced in France during that period. He contrasts that productivity with the paucity of production during the moralistic Gaullist repression of the 1960s. (Of German, Italian, and Japanese stag production we have been unable to discover much reliable information, and if the present analysis tends to focus on the United States and France, it is due less to chauvinist intentions than to the available information about a highly fugitive genre. For more on this problem see the section on International Vistas.)

Kyrou ties the decrease of French stag production in his time to the closing of the brothels and houses of assignation (*maisons closes* and *maisons de passes*) in which film showings were officially tolerated. He notes that one of the most prolific stag *auteurs*—*le célèbre* Dominique—remained unharassed by the police because he limited his sales of films to *mauvais lieux* ("bad places"). In America no such *auteur* emerged, although several series and groups of individual films demonstrated common stylistic idiosyncracies and affinities (not unlike the short plays that comprise medieval mystery cycles). Since brothels were irregularly tolerated and haphazardly organized in the United States, they did not provide the obvious setting for the showing of stag films. For almost four decades—from the twenties into the fifties—the largest market for stag films in America remained men-only "smokers" or "stag parties," and the audience most commonly belonged to two kinds of male groups: upper-lower and lower-middle-class voluntary social organizations (Legionnaires, Shriners, Elks, etc.), and residential college students, usually those in fraternities. Although officially illegal, these showings were invariably tolerated in their individual communities as a necessary ritual of masculine emergence. (In Bloomington, Indiana, the local Legion even announced their next stag screening in the hometown newspaper.) The law not only turned a blind eye to these occasions, but even participated. Policemen, in particular, often having access to confiscated prints, shared in the stag rituals.

During the twenties and thirties when projection equipment was cumbersome, stag screenings were primarily road-show operations. Usually the dealer provided a sixteen-millimeter projector and enough reels for two or three hours of viewing for a flat fee of fifty to one hundred dollars. Throughout the forties and well into the fifties fraternal organizations were the commonest audiences for stag films. With the decrease in the cost of projection equipment and the development of eight-millimeter technology, however, home viewing increasingly replaced the communal smoker. The outright sale of films to private collectors began to surpass road-show rentals. As the porno film emerged, the stag smoker declined further, although in certain sections of the country, among certain classes, the rituals continue.

Certain aspects of the American stag are elucidated by examining its audience and circumstances of viewing. Sociologists John Gagnon and William Simon have pointed out that the stag rituals helped acculturate the American male by meeting several needs. In an era in which the "facts of life" were garnered haphazardly, the films offered detailed instructions in sexual technique and expressed vital collective heterosexual concerns. For the college male the stag film represented a shared experience which affirmed his developing sexuality. By facing the traumas of sexual initiation with collective bravado ("Hey Joe, look at the jugs on that broad"), the collegian showed his peers that he had survived the rites of sexual passage. The films revealed graphically what it was difficult to see in the dark confines of the back seat. Similarly, one of the obsessive conventions of the stag film—the low-angle shot of penis entering vagina in missionary position—had several functions. It illustrated the myth of male dominance (man literally over woman); it showed the viewer that he was getting his money's worth, that no simulation was involved; it provided an essential anatomy lesson not present in available textbooks. The stag film showed

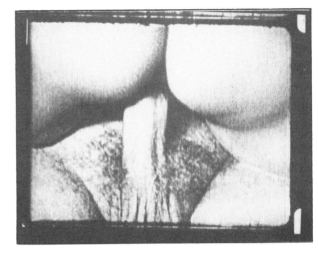

Slow-Fire Dentist, 1920's.

55

the college male what he dared not ask his peers for fear of acknowledging inexperience.

For the other, older group, exposure to stag films usually came later in life, after marriage or after the firm establishment of sexual patterns. For this audience the films provided a similar experience of male bonding, not so much as a rite of adolescent passage but as a validation of appetites society had forced it to publicly reject. For groups with severe sanctions against extra-marital sex, for

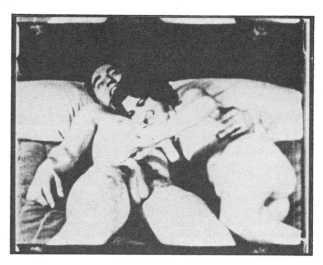

Hot Party, 1928-1933.

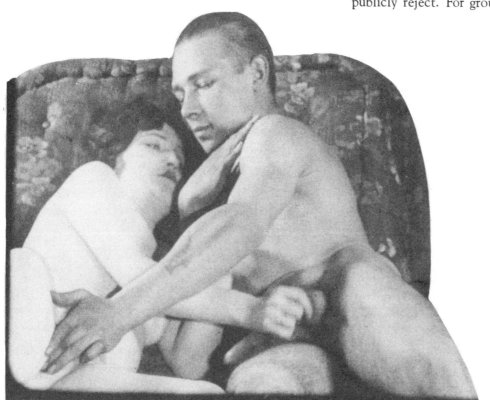

56

Wonders of the Unseen World, 1927.

middle-aged men fearful or incapable of exploring forbidden sexual terrain, the films affirmed their existence as sexual creatures and as men. The films further reinforced the obsessive myths of male sexual fantasy: a real man can have any woman; all women want to be dominated sexually; sex can happen anytime anywhere; human beings are universal sexual tinder. As Gagnon and Simon write: "The group viewer is able to prove he knows the language of sexuality—a language he can't use elsewhere. . . . The need for this approbation of his fellows is at least as strong as his need for approbation from women."

The inter-titles of the earlier stags often explicitly reinforce these social and instructional qualities. They offer ego reassurance: "Men are men in the open spaces," accompanies the sexual activities of the stud in *A Free Ride*. "Gals, do you think it's big enough?" asks the proud hero of his two appreciative female companions in *A Trip to Pleasure Island*. "What a man," reads a title in *Matinee Idol*, "he's coming back for more."

Through the medium of broad humor the films offer lessons in sexual technique. As the hero of *Strictly Union*—Hard Penis—fingers the vagina of an aspiring extra, the title reads: "Stink finger. The quickest known method for heating purposes." In *Slow-fire Dentist*, the titular hero revives a gassed patient by vaginal massage, which is described as "a new way to revive them." He then undresses her, lays her on a cot and fucks her side-ways: "A New Method." A French film, *The Chiropodist*, has clearly been embellished by American titles: "Take it easy and keep it greasy, then it slips in very easy, for it's good to the last drop." *Casting Couch* points out that "a little cold cream does a lot of good sometimes." And in a film most aptly named *Wonders of the Unseen World*, the inter-titles abound in instructional description: "Belly to belly," "Old fashion way [sic] which has long been out of use" (missionary position), "Cowboy Fashion," "The New Way," and "The latest importation from Paris" (cunnilingus).

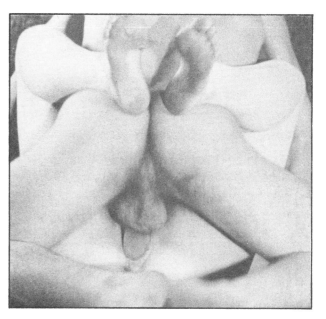

Wonders of the Unseen World, 1927.

57

The films often offer moral as well as anatomical and technical instruction. *Wonders of the Unseen World* ends by asking, "Put yourselves in their place, and what would you have done?" *Strictly Union* offers the familiar aphorism, "A stiff prick has no conscience." *A Free Ride* affirms sex without guilt—"All's well that ends well"—and *The Goat*, which recounts a practical joke played by some girls on the hero, warns that the world of sex has its pitfalls—"Watch your step because there's one born every second." The films are aware they flout official morality but suffer no guilt in doing so. They accept the primacy of sexual claims and the flimsiness of barriers to their fulfillment.

"A Peeping Tom." *The Pick Up,* 1923.

"'BYE, 'BYE MISS AMERICAN PIE"

THE AMERICAN STAG FILM was constant in its essentials through five decades; despite a few double-reelers and occasional late experiments with color and synchronized sound, it remained largely a silent, one-reel form. Nonetheless it evolved distinctly—or, more accurately—

The Goat, 1920-1926.

The ocean has been encroaching upon the land at the rate of one inch a year — — an inch means more in some places than in others.

retrogressed. Despite their reliance upon performers often drawn from the worlds of prostitution and procurement, the films of the teens, twenties, and thirties displayed narrative and stylistic concerns which almost totally disappeared after the Second World War. Most of the extant early films display an expertise that suggests that at the outset the stag film received the attention of professionals, a condition which progressively diminished in its subsequent history. This professionalism was understandable in an era in which film equipment was expensive and cumbersome, hence unavailable to the amateur.

The films of the teens and early twenties reveal a distinctive style. They are often shot out-of-doors or in specifically defined settings (movie studio, dentist's office, etc.); they build up to sex through narrative situations. They comment extensively on the action through inter-titles, and, most characteristically, they display almost universally a broad, vulgar humor rooted in sexual and scatological folklore. In *Strictly Union* (1919), for example, the principal characters are Hard Penis, Minnie Womb, and Lotta Crap; the action takes place at the Fuckem

Right Movie Studios. These "dirty" names represent the kind of adolescent, obscene humor evident in such "book titles" as *The Open Kimona* by Seymour Hare, *The Hole in the Bed* by Mr. Completely, and *The African Maid* by Erasmus B. Black, and apparent in such other obscene folklore as spooneristic conundrums ("What's the difference between a lawyer and an angry hen? An angry hen clucks defiance."), wanton daughter puns ("She was only a wrestler's daughter, but you ought to see her box."), and Confucianisms ("Confucius say, 'Man who screws in graveyard is fucking near dead.' "). The raunchy humor unites the stag film with the deep undercurrent of obscenity once prohibited in polite language but acknowledged on the street corner; the stag draws on the raw power of that part of the folk tradition suppressed in Anglo-Saxon culture after the expurgation of the jestbooks in the 1830s. Since this tradition is defiantly anti-genteel, the grosser the obscenity the better. Dirty names are used not only for the characters in the early films but for their pseudonymous film makers as well. The credits for one film read: "Seduced by A. Prick, Directed by Ima Cunt, Photographed by R. U. Hard." The tradition, somewhat tamed, continues into the pornos.

Few American stags derive their subject matter from literary pornography. The exception that proves this rule is *An English Tragedy* (1920-26), based upon a British Victorian sado-masochistic novel, *The Way of a Man with a Maid*. The inter-titles are floridly literary rather than vulgar: "The day of reckoning has come. You amused yourself with my heart, I am going to amuse myself with your body." This melodramatic dialogue is, however, atypical, American stag film makers preferring popular to literary sources.

The communal nature of the smoker encouraged the use of vulgar humor by defusing the anxieties produced by the moral sanctions defied and the powerful, forbidden sexual imagery. The films were elaborate dirty jokes and could be laughed at. Indeed, several early films are either based upon dirty jokes or use a

"Moral—Watch your step because there's one born every second."
The Goat, 1920-1926.

The Goat, 1920-1926.

"Anthony Browning was so idle that he believed in fairies and mermaids."

"Let's take a swim—there ain't a soul around!"

"An eye-full is better than an earful."

"Your clothes back and ten dollars."

"Everything will have to be done right through here!"

"That's the best girl I ever had in all my life!"

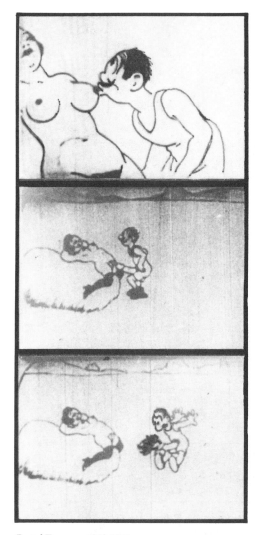

Buried Treasure, 1928-1933.

joke as the mainspring of their narrative. *The Pick Up* (1923) not only illustrates a well-known dirty joke but includes in its inter-titles short gags and double entendres: "It's probably silly but we wonder if you've heard about the girl who stepped out with a taxidermist and then played DEAD." The hero is introduced: "GUS—the man who broke Solomon's home into a thousand PIECES." (Even if this title is embellished by the drawing of an erect penis, it assumes some biblical familiarity.) The film recounts how the rakish Gus picks up Lizzie the flapper in his car, drives her out of town, and makes his pitch:

"Anything doing, baby?"

"How far are we from town?" she asks.

"Ten miles."

"NO."

"GET OUT!"

She gets out docilely, waves goodbye, and walks off towards town.

The next day the events reoccur, and twenty miles from town she still says "NO." However, on the anecdotally conventional third go-round, this time fifty miles from town, she succumbs and they have sex. Afterwards, Gus asks why she was reluctant earlier.

"I don't mind walking ten, fifteen, or twenty miles," she replies, "but I'll be damned if I'll walk fifty, just to keep you—" (Close-up of her; new inter-title) "—from getting a dose of CLAPP [*sic*]!!"

The film is well made, with varied set-ups (long, medium, close, reverse shots, a moving shot of the car), and, for the genre, is crisply edited. This professionalism is also apparent in *The Goat* (a.k.a. *Getting His Goat*, 1920-26), whose plot is a traditional folk motif—the practical joke of substituting something undesirable for the sexually anticipated. It also begins with an off-color aphorism: "The ocean has been encroaching upon the land at the rate of one inch a year—an inch means more in some places than in others." The story opens as a young man, idling by a seaside fence, spies three attractive women completely undress in preparation for a swim. He has an erection, confronts them, and they run away. Undeterred, he confiscates their clothes, then negotiates for their favors. They agree that for fifty dollars he can have his pick, but he has to make his choice through a knothole in the fence. He puts his hand through and fingers each girl in turn, smelling his finger after each digital insertion. Then he fantasizes about having sex with each. He thrusts his penis through the knothole. The women spy a goat, back it up to the fence, and the young man ecstactically fucks it. The girls reappear dressed, one with an apparently swollen belly. They demand more money, and as they leave, the "pregnant" girl removes a pillow and throws it at the dupe. They raise their dresses and flash their asses in a gesture of contempt as our chastened hero staggers and collapses.

The penchant for obscene farce found a perfect vehicle in the more difficult but imaginatively unfettered form of the animated cartoon, which had developed a violent, frenetic, quasi-surrealist, distinctly American style in the 1920s. The years 1921-28 were the golden age of Otto Messmer's Felix the Cat. Felix lives in a perennially delightful fantasyland unadorned by anything except essential props and a few distinguishing landmarks. It is a malleable environment because Felix assumes the artist's power to alter its outlines if necessary. His emotions are as tangible as any object; he reaches up to catch exclamation points that issue from his head and converts them into baseball bats or airplane propellers. He is also aware of his own arbitrary reality, the sometimes warring, sometimes helpful, independence of his physical parts. His tail, for example, is detachable, useful as a cane or umbrella, but often recalcitrant.

The sexual possibilities of Felix's animated fantasyland were apparent to the skilled, anonymous creator of *Buried Treasure*, the most famous of several porno-

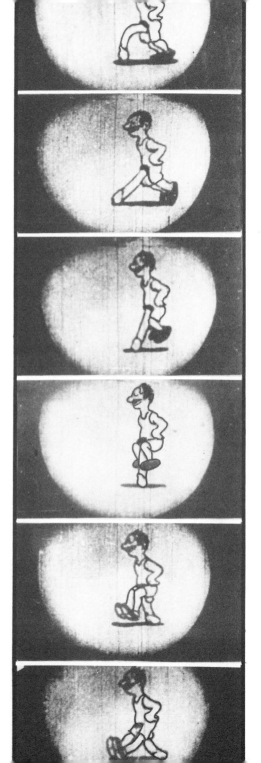

Buried Treasure, 1928-1933.

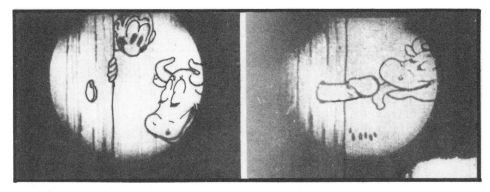

Buried Treasure, 1928-1933.

graphic animated cartoons to emerge in the late twenties or early thirties. Heavily indebted to Messmer's simple style, *Buried Treasure* is less concerned with its hero Everready's detachable tail than with his independent penis. The film concretizes the theme of lust's overwhelming power—the prick has a life of its own. At the beginning of the film Everready shoots an annoying fly from his enormous penis with a gun. After the explosion he is appalled to find the penis gone. He spies it peeking out from behind a rock, beckons it back, and as it resumes its customary place, he gives it a reassuring pat. Later, after thrusting his penis into the crowded vagina of a seductive woman (he removes a shoe and a clock before proceeding), he pulls out to find a crab clutching the sensitive head. Again, the outraged penis flees such ill treatment and agrees to return only after considerable cajoling. The aptly named Everready then mistakenly thrusts into the anus of a man buried beneath a sandhill that covers a lovely woman. Everready runs away appalled, but his penis remains stuck; it stretches and stretches, dragging the protesting man along, until it detaches and recoils with such ferocity that it sends him flying. Still later, Everready and an outraged Mexican (who will

Buried Treasure, 1928-1933.

not share the ecstatic donkey he has been screwing) duel energetically with clashing penises. *Buried Treasure* is consistently amusing because it fully exploits the power of animation to delineate a logic photography can only suggest: when men are led by their pricks, they have problems as well as pleasures. The penile burden is occasionally so heavy that it would seem a wheelbarrow is necessary to carry it around.

The tradition of broad sexual humor continued into the 1930s. In *Matinee Idol* Blondie Blondell is seduced by Lord Fuckem of Fuckem, Fuckem, and Fuckem, Ltd., "sole agents for Everip Cundrums," and in *A Stiff Game* Bill Hangnuts "decides to participate in a hot game of dominoes at the Blow Girls Club." Although *Matinee Idol* offers such major characters as a British lord, a London show girl, and her "little London maid," the treatment is pure, raunchy, scatological burlesque in an American farcical tradition. "Wee Wampus," Blondie's maid, who is anything but wee, informs Lord Fuckem that Blondie is out and will return soon from her drive with Sir Rattling Nuts. Wee decides to "vamp" his Lordship by shooting her powerful "tit-rays" at him. He succumbs, they wrestle, he falls

Buried Treasure, 1928-1933.

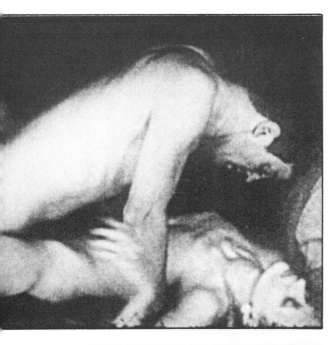

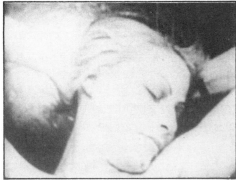

Matinee Idol, 1930's.

back and Wee grabs him and blows him. As he prepares to mount her he grimaces: "Whew! Is that a dead horse?" The camera pans to Wee's chamber pot in which is a large turd. His Lordship dismisses the distraction and leaps on Wee. While they are fucking Blondie returns and is peeved: "Oh, I say your Lordship, you cawn't do that, you know." Lord Fuckem immediately directs his attention to the attractive Blondie. Wee exits angrily: "Nuts to your Lordship!" Blondie undresses and "turns on her heat" by gyrating provocatively on the bed. They fuck; he comes on her belly, whereupon she turns on MORE HEAT. More fucking. "Believe it or not his Lordship is slowing down." But after a third encounter it is Blondie, not his indefatigable Lordship, who is "out on the third strike."

Although *A Stiff Game* continues the tradition of obscene humor, it is atypical in other respects. It acknowledges the social reality of the Depression and includes scenes of homosexual, black-white sex in an essentially heterosexual film. It opens on a park bench with the hero, Bill Hangnuts, reading a newspaper, obviously scanning the want-ads. He is "disgusted of being out of work and decides to seek his living in an easier and more pleasurable manner." There follows a long shot of Bill walking down the street of a medium-sized, not easily identifiable, city. We cut to a room where Bill and a black man, Sambo the porter, are "well at work in a stiff game." A high-angle shot of the two men shooting craps follows; Sambo loses and removes his pants and shoes. As Bill removes his shorts in turn, Sambo grabs Bill's penis and begins to fellate him. "Sambo loses the game but wins the bologna. . . But collects heavy on some white meat and hair pie." A girl enters, lies down, and Sambo turns his attention to her. As he performs cunnilingus, the inter-title ironically comments: "He was later disqualified by the KKK." (This can be read as an *anti*-racist remark, for despite his minstrel name, throughout the film Sambo is an equal sexual particip-

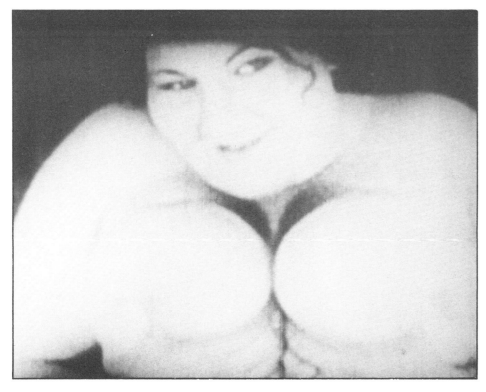

"Shooting her 'Tit-Rays' at his Lordship." *Matinee Idol,* 1930's.

ant.) The sex escalates as another woman enters. "So Bill finds the game growing stiffer and the Players change positions." The varied sexual activity—now all heterosexual—includes one woman drinking Bill's urine from a glass. Finally, the "moral": "Sambo was down and Bill was out, which left the girls with a tasty mouth."

"Starring the famous Blondie Blondell Direct From The London Gaiety Theatre . . . And Here She Is"

67

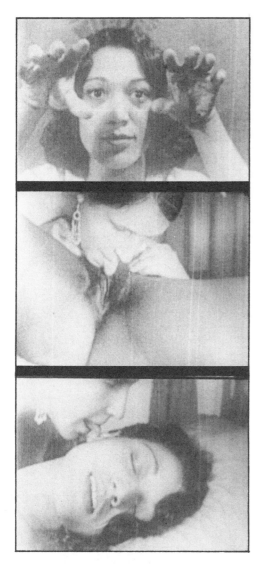

"Madame Cyprian who is getting ready for a seance."
The Hypnotist, 1932-1936.

The 1930s stag films increasingly tired of the Lord Fuckem school of obscene verbal humor, preferring to achieve their erotic effects through dramatic situation and action rather than humorous comment. Both *The Hypnotist* and *The Modern Magician*, for example, shot in attractive interiors, concentrated on the seductive possibilities of the professions involved in their titles. In *The Hypnotist*, Madame Cyprian, through her skill, seduces a woman and a man in turn, after which they participate in a threesome. Although the film indicates the future direction of the stag by deemphasizing elements peripheral to sex, it is carefully shot and selectively edited. *The Modern Magician* is not devoid of humor either. Its hero, "the Great Hokum," performs such specialties as the "detachable prick trick," but he soon abandons his trickery for the real thing. His energetic lovemaking with a lovely blonde—the same girl who played Blondie Blondell—is attractively shot with but one final titular salute to the superiority of sexual reality to illusion: "Oh boy! That's magic!"

The increase of a surface sophistication in setting and narrative situation, mirroring trends in the open cinema, is evident in the late thirties film *Adventures Abroad*. In a sumptous art deco interior two girls lounge about, their phone rings, one girl answers and announces that "it's Lulu, just back from her trip abroad." After a fade out, a well-dressed woman enters and embraces her friends. Lulu takes a globe and points out where she has been. The film then presents a series of vignettes in which the girls improvise sexual variations based on different national tastes and styles: one rides another in "cossack" fashion, "Paree" suggests energetic cunnilingus, and, finally, in "The Dictator's Special," the three girls touch each other's vaginas, *Heil* Hitler, and simulate his moustache with their wet fingers. The contrast between the sophistication of the costumes and setting and the gross overtness of the women's behavior is revealing. As a lesbian film for a male audience it is concerned with carefully displaying the "unseen wonders" of the female genitalia. The women may look sophisticated but essentially they are whores, sticking cigarettes in their vaginas, spreading themselves for view, falling back with their asses high. Despite the avoidance of verbal grossness, the traditional values of the stag still pertain.

After the Second World War the conditions of stag production and distribution changed and the films changed with them. The greater availability of sixteen-millimeter equipment enabled the stag to move from the communal smoker to the privacy of the living room or den. Although the men who had organized the road shows for two decades became the first distributors, wholesalers, and retailers of the new market, the proliferation of relatively inexpensive cameras and projectors permitted the entry of amateur competitors. With the development of eight-millimeter technology the diffusion of stag production increased further. By the mid-fifties, as pornographic series surfaced in such places as Detroit, Nashville, and Dallas, the quality of the films plummeted. Not only did humor decline—and almost disappear—but nearly all attempts at film structure collapsed as well. In these films there were as few narrative preliminaries as possible:

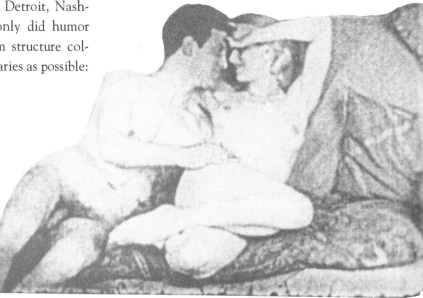

The Modern Magician, 1930's.

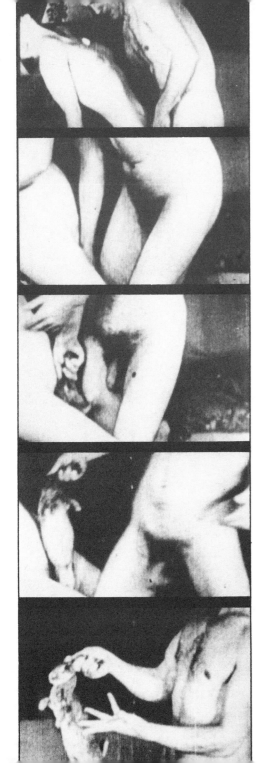

sexual activity became the exclusive concern. A hotel or motel room, two performers, a camera and a roll of film were all that were needed. The performers, invariably lower class, were almost completely without their predecessors' energy or enthusiasm. The men were more frequently disguised, and this was the period in which they often removed everything but their socks.

The major technical concern of this period was to avoid wasting film. The shooting ratio was as close to one-to-one as possible; there were few out-takes. Even failures of sexual performance, primarily male flaccidness, were not excised. Technical errors—bad framing, misfocus, useless footage, etc.—remained unedited. These filmic conditions continued into the sixties. About the only technological development seized upon was the use of zoom-lenses, which enabled film makers to move from medium shots to close-ups without varying the set-up. Synchronized sound was still virtually absent, though color appeared with greater frequency.

One major series, probably produced in the east in the late 1940s and early 1950s, heralded a transition in the postwar stag: the *Merry-Go-Round-Emergency Clinic* series. The series, comprising over thirty films with such titles as *Night School,* *The Dentist,* and *Varsity Girls,* demonstrated the prolific, assembly-line methods of the new stag producers. Several of the films, however, continued to exploit the slapstick humor of the prewar era: in *The Emergency Clinic* a horny girl uses increasingly larger dildos until a huge one gets stuck. She is rushed to a clinic where two young doctors playfully examine her with outsized instruments. They finally remove the dildo, give the girl an aphrodisiac, and have sex with her. In general, however, this burlesque humor was a dying style. Most of the remaining films in the series were distinguished primarily by the frequent appearance of the same male "superstar," a performer who seemed to enjoy demeaning his female sex partners.

"The rabbit out of the box." *The Modern Magician,* 1930's.

A *Stiff Game*, 1930's.

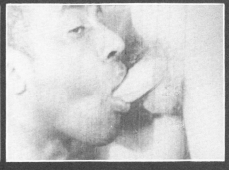

"He decides to participate in a hot game of dominoes at Blow Girl's Club."

"Two hours later Bill and Sambo the porter well at work at a stiff game."

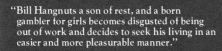

"Bill Hangnuts a son of rest, and a born gambler for girls becomes disgusted of being out of work and decides to seek his living in an easier and more pleasurable manner."

"Sambo loses the game but wins the balogna. But collects heavy on the white meat and hair pie."

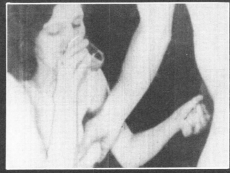

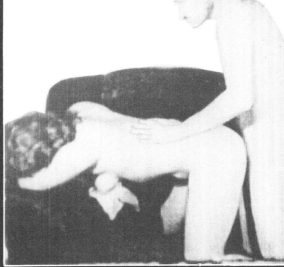

"Morals: Sambo was down and Bill was out, which left the girls with a tasty mouth."

71

The Handy Man, 1930's.

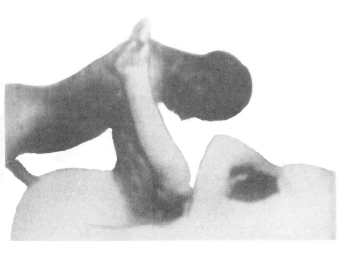

"Yes, did you bring your tool?" *The Handy Man,* 1930's.

The one film from this postwar period that merits special attention may well be the single most popular film of the genre—*Smart Aleck.* It represents the one known stag film to star a "name" performer, the stripper Candy Barr. At the time of its production in Dallas in 1951, however, she was a sixteen-year-old named Juanita Slusher. In a recent interview in *Oui* magazine, Ms. Barr maintains that although she was not forced to make the film, she did not exactly choose to do so either: "I never thought about doing it. I wasn't Candy Barr then. But it happened and I've had a lot of flack about it. People say, 'What the hell, it's only a fuck movie.' Well, that was 1951; I *do* care what the hell. If I had done it by choice, then I would have had some mechanism to adjust it into my lifestyle. But I didn't do it by choice. . . . I wasn't lured. I was taken, done and that was it."

It is surely true that much of Ms. Barr's subsequent harassment by the law (a twenty-year sentence, of which she served three years, for marijuana possession) stemmed from her dubious celebrity-status as the first pornographic star and her consequent role (like her contemporary Lenny Bruce) as a symbolic subverter of official morality. *Smart Aleck,* however, is distinguished only—perhaps sufficiently—by her youthful presence. It is a motel film *par excellence.* A travelling salesman invites Candy into his motel room from the swimming pool. He plies her with liquor and makes his move. They engage in sex. The only "dramatic" moment occurs when Candy refuses to go down on him. (Ms. Barr comments: "At the time I wasn't even aware that people engaged in oral sex. . . . It wasn't something I'd planned to make part of my life.") To placate him, she calls in a girl friend who performs the forbidden act, and Candy rejoins the action in more conventional ways.

Ms. Barr's notoriety raises the perennial question of whether such Hollywood stars as Joan Crawford, Greta Garbo, or Marilyn Monroe appeared in stag films. It is not impossible, of course, that sitting in the vaults of some producer or wealthy collector lie some of these mythic films. But the two largest American stag collections (those of the ISR and a well-known publisher) contain no such items. We are reminded of the tattoo artist's myth of the fox hunt, in which a man's back is completely covered with hunters and hounds pursuing a fox whose tail is disappearing up the man's anus. No one has actually *seen* the fox hunt, but there is always a friend who has. Similarly, someone else has always actually seen Joan Crawford's blue film. There is evidence, however, that pornographic scenes were spliced into such thirties films as *Red Dust* and *Camille* for showing in the "specialized" cinemas of Latin America, with look-alikes finishing what Harlow and Garbo started. Recently, the peep show tenderloin in New York City has displayed stag films ostensibly starring Jayne Mansfield and Barbra Streisand. The "Jayne Mansfield" film is so unclear as to defy identification, but the "Streisand" film, supposedly shot in Greenwich Village in the sixties, does offer an enthusias-

Two French Wildcats, 1930's.

73

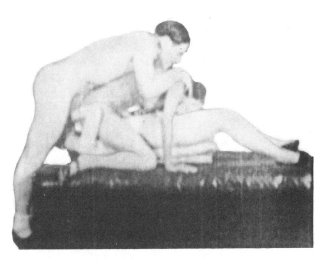

The Hypnotist, 1932-1936.

tic heroine who looks very much as Barbra must have looked a decade ago. In the absence of any corroborating evidence, however, we continue to stand on the fox hunt theory.

By the mid-1960s changing sexual values and improved technology created a partial resurgence in stag quality, at least in cinematography, looks, and performance, if not in narrative or thematic development. Prior to World War II stag performers clearly reflected the clandestine world of the sexual underground: many female performers were prostitutes. They were not young; some were even middle-aged, and their male companions were even older. After the war performers were drawn increasingly from a broader social spectrum. The distinction between the saved and the damned continued to erode, and both male and female performers were younger and more attractive, many having no association with the world of commercialized vice. The step to the porno starlet was not far off.

A series of films produced in New York City in the mid-1960s with such titles as *Village Ball, Pajama Game, Love Nest,* and *Swinging Hotel* featured performers drawn from the bohemian-drug fringe who were relatively attractive, animated, and sexually adventurous. In *Village Ball,* shot in color and in two reels, one woman transfers ejaculate into the mouth of another, an action which occasionally occurs in the pornos and peeps but which was unheard of in the classic stag. The films reveal the growing substitution of group sex for the traditional one-on-one encounters of earlier films. (*Love Nest* features one male and three females; *Wild Night* two males and three females; and *Swinging Hotel* two males and four females.) These films represent a direct line to the pornos (particularly the New York brand) which were soon to emerge. Although other series were produced in the sixties in such unlikely film capitals as Detroit and rural Indiana, they lacked the technical expertise of their big-city rivals.

INTERNATIONAL VISTAS: FRENCH, ENGLISH, NO GREEK

ALTHOUGH MORE STAG FILMS were probably produced in the United States than any other country for economic and technological reasons, we cannot say so with certainty. As already noted, the stag emerged first in France, where it flourished (except during the Second World War) until the Gaullist repression. Kyrou also documents an extensive series of films produced in Vienna in the twenties, none of which, to my knowledge, have surfaced in America. That a body of Japanese stag films exists is confirmed by the publicly released Japanese film of the late sixties, *The Pornographer*, which centers on a man who makes stags for a wholesaler to distribute to private collectors. Although the film implies that a considerable private pornographic industry has existed in Japan for some time, in the American-market through 1970 few films with Oriental principals can definitively be traced to the Far East. (In the 1970s films clearly shot in Cambodia or Vietnam, before the American exodus, and in Pakistan or India have appeared in the peep arcades.)

Despite the *lingua franca* of the silent stag form and the absence of copyrights and royalties, the evidence suggests that because of legal dangers, customs restrictions, and the safer, regional nature of stag distribution, most of a country's production was not seen outside its borders. The stag film did not travel well. This is not to maintain that *no* interchange of films occurred; the American market offered considerable foreign material, primarily Latin American and French. Among the very few films released with bi-lingual inter-titles were *El*

Adventures Abroad, 1930's.

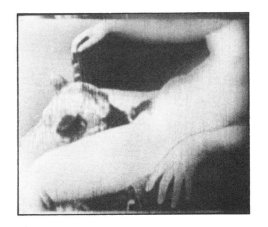

Mexican Dog, 1930's.

75

Adventures Abroad, 1930's.

"It's Lulu, just back from her trip abroad..."

"Hey—what about Paree?"

"Now—I'll show you the Dictator's Special."

Perro Masajista (a.k.a. "Mexican Dog"), and a Viennese film with French title *Cabinet Particulier* ("Private Room," 1928), released with joint French and English titles. Clearly, the Mexican and Cuban films in particular were intended as much for American as for local consumption. Kyrou's filmography also shows that Italian and Spanish, as well as American, films surfaced in France, and that in the mid-thirties a high quality stag series was jointly produced in France and Germany. Of pre-World War II German stag production we have been unable to find enough information to generalize. Despite the assumption that the stag flourished in the Weimar Republic and Julius Streicher's notorious penchant for pornography, few German films appeared on the American market and none (exclusive of the Austrian) are cited in Kyrou's filmography.

The following analysis is, then, inevitably selective. The four groups of international stags with which we are familiar are (1) the Latin American (Mexican, Cuban) film of the 1930s through the 1950s; (2) the French film of the 1920s through the 1950s; (3) the British film of the 1960s; and (4) the post-legalization Scandinavian (Danish, Swedish) film of the late 1960s and beyond. Since the stag era may be said to end with the advent of the American porno in 1970, we shall focus primarily on the earlier, pre-1970 Scandinavian films. The form of the short, silent pornographic film of course continues, and we shall deal with this continuity later.

The archetypal Latin American film derives from the whorehouse. Most Mexican and Cuban films seem to have been produced in the flourishing brothels of Tijuana and pre-Castro Havana. The performers are obviously from the world of procurement. The males are often those who played stud roles in live whorehouse exhibitions. The females, often quite young, provoke sympathy for their apparent sexual victimization. Bestiality is common fare in such films as *Rin Tin Tin Mexicano*, *A Hunter and His Dog*, *Rascal Rex*, and *El Perro Masajista*. In

Mexican Dog, 1930's.

Farmer's Daughter, 1930's.

the latter film a man who seems almost a guard successively admits three women into a room to have sex with a dog who, contrary to the film's title, displays no masochistic proclivities. The technical quality of the films is invariably poor. Their distinctive themes are the humiliation and subservience of women, and anticlericalism. Several films have sequences in which priests exploit their authority for sexual advantage (for example, *Mexican Honeymoon*). Since pornography has historically objectified the violations of social taboos, anticlerical pornography has flourished in countries in which the authority and imagery of the church—almost exclusively the Catholic Church—has been powerful. The American stag film is remarkably free of religious subject matter. The one apparent exception, *The Nun's Story* (1949-50), surfaced under the alternate title *College Coed*, a transformation which indicates either a naive or conscious confusion of religious habit and academic regalia. Protestantism has never provided the iconography hospitable to erotic transformation.

Along with the United States, France has produced the most extensive body of stag material, and, thanks to Ado Kyrou and Lo Duca, much of it is documented. Kyrou notes the existence of two *auteurs* of the French stag film who prospered in the 1920s: the aforementioned Dominique, and Bernard Nathan. Producing films for *maisons closes* and *maisons de passes*, they functioned semi-openly. Nathan's films (in which he generally played the leading role) cover a wide range of subjects and milieus. He was particularly fond of historical and exotic subjects in such films as *Les Filles de Loth* ("Lot's Daughters," 1920), *Madame Butterfly* (1920), *Musique de Chambre* ("Chamber Music," 1922)—in which Madame Pompadour is a character, *Tournée des Grand-Ducs* ("The Rounds of the Grand Dukes," 1923), and *Mecktoub* (1925), one of two Nathan films we know of to surface in America. In *Mecktoub* Dick, a photographer, is introduced into the seraglio of Sheik D'Abd-El-Zob during his absence to take some pictures of the female occupants. He is not content with photos and is surprised by the

"**The star pupil.**" *Hycock's Dancing School,* 1932-1936.

master of the harem as he is giving erotic lessons to some of the girls. As punishment Dick is forced to keep photographing while the sheik, his body guards, and two of the harem girls cavort sexually before him. He is then unceremoniously expelled.

The indefatigable Nathan did not limit himself to exotic subject matter, however. He made several outdoor films, such as *Le Beau Champignon* ("The Nice Mushroom"), *Le Moine* ("The Monk"—but it is not about a monk), and *Je Verbalise* ("I Make a Report"—the other Nathan film available in American collections), in which ordinary people—gardeners, farmers, hunters, laundresses, gamekeepers—engage in sexual variations which include the bisexual.

Dominique, for the most part, did not share Nathan's exotic tastes, although he did produce films about *Le Prince et le Groom* (1924) and theatrical aristocracy. In *Pendant l'Entr'acte* ("During the Intermission," 1921), "Sarah Barnum" finds a

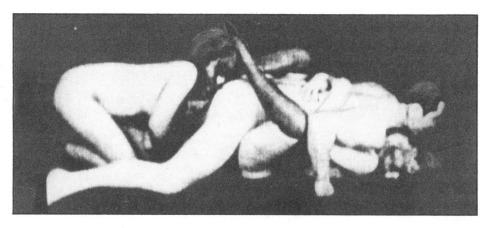

"**The new arrival makes it an adagio trio.**" *Hycock's Dancing School,* 1932-1936.

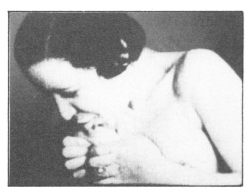

Hycock's Dancing School, 1932-1936.

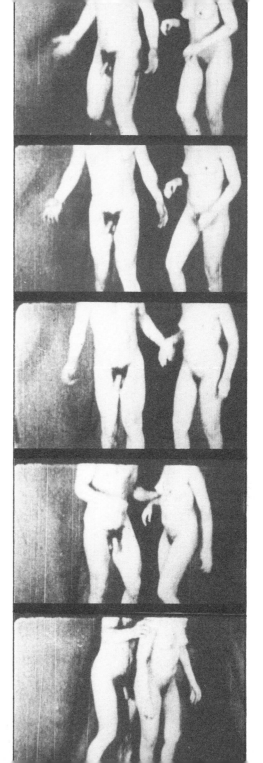

gentleman behind a screen in her dressingroom and makes the most of his presence with the assistance of her maid. Dominique's films painted an erotic panorama of French working life, with characters drawn from diverse occupations. The titles demonstrate his social range: *Le Peintre, A la Cuisine, Le Coiffeur, Après la Classe, La Nouvelle Bonne a tout faire* ("Maid of All Work"), *Les Modistes.* Dominique seemed determined to produce a sexual *comédie humaine.* Not having seen his films, we cannot attest to their quality, but Kyrou's scenarios reveal a strain of humor more ironic than broad in the American tradition, and a penchant for sexual complication. He rarely shot a scene with only two participants, a characteristic which contrasts sharply with American films of the same period.

It seems apparent that French film makers were working for a more sophisticated audience than the Americans. *Titres cocasses* ("humorous titles") are not nearly as omnipresent as in the early American stag, though wry humor is common. French films of the twenties and thirties were much more exotic in theme and setting than their American counterparts and resisted the temptation to subordinate plot and story line to purely sexual activity. Interestingly, one national stereotype is confirmed by the French stags: many associate sex with food and drink, for example, *La Cueillette des Olives* ("The Olive Gathering"), *La Voleuse de Prunes* ("The Girl Who Steals Prunes"), *A la Cuisine* ("In the Kitchen"), *La Beau Champignon, Un Apéritif Bien Servi.* Food is rare in American stags, although its waste products occasionally figure prominently. As a French friend once replied to complaints about Gallic toilets: *"Alors, en France on mange bien; en Amérique on chie bien. C'est une petite différence de tempérament."* ("Well, in France you eat well; in America you shit well. It's a small difference in temperament.")

As one would expect in a Catholic country, anticlericalism is evident in such films as *Les Mystères du Couvent* ("Mysteries of the Convent," 1928), and *Messe Noire* ("Black Mass," 1928), though it is not as widespread as one might think. One of the few startling moments in stag films is a moment of blasphemy which occurs in a film known on the American market as *A Bare Interlude* (1928-33) but which seems to be of French origin. In the film's final sequence, the heroine, who has had her pubic hair shaved and her male companion's arm thrust into her vagina almost to the elbow, sits on a table nude except for a hat. The table is set with three glasses and three plates on which are three fish and three slices of bread. The other places remain empty. When she finishes eating the fish, she steps up on the table and urinates into the three glasses, filling them. The film ends. There is a surreal, Buñuelesque quality to the sequence and to the entire film.

This surreal structure may be accidental rather than consciously intended. Professor Hoffman argues convincingly in the filmography in *Analytical Survey of Anglo-American Traditional Erotica* that the absence of narrative line or clear

Confidential Circus, 1930-1935.

82

"You are now at a side show and will see the great feats of passion performed. Dot, Flo, and Willie." *Confidential Circus,* 1930-1935.

chronology in the extant American version may have resulted if the original film were smuggled into the country in pieces and then respliced haphazardly. Whether intentional or aleatoric, *A Bare Interlude* is atypically distinctive.

All but halted by the Second World War, the French stag emerged vigorously in the late forties and fifties and thrived until dampened by De Gaulle. The contemporaneous esthetic decline of the American stag was not duplicated, perhaps one reason being that the amateur photography revolution did not as soon occur. Several 1950's French films, in fact, are among the most imaginative of the genre, in particular *Petit Conte de Noël* (1950) and *La Femme au Portrait* (1952). The former title contains an obscene French pun (*conte de, con de*) which permits it to be translated either as "A Little Christmas Story" or "A Little Christmas Cunt." The plot involves a disconsolate young girl who finds herself on Christmas Eve alone and horny. A masked Santa Claus appears and asks what is wrong. The girl replies that no one loves her, and in a flashback we see her governess rejecting the girl's advances. Generous Santa consoles her by producing an elaborate fucking machine in which a dildo is propelled by bicycle pedals.

"A sister act." *Hycock's Dancing School*, 1932-1936.

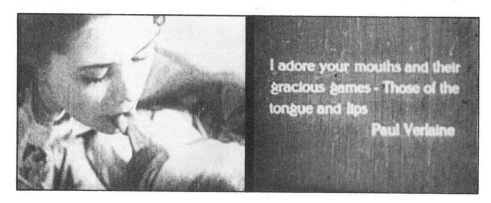

"The coitus of the tongues." *Torture of Tickling Tongues*, 1930-1935.

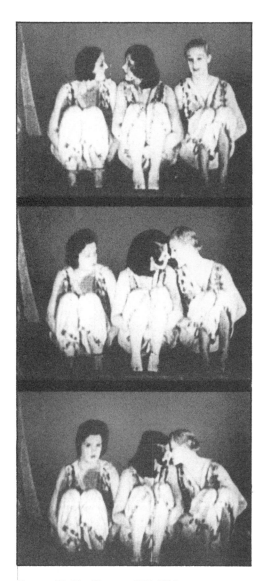

Torture of Tickling Tongues, 1930-1935.

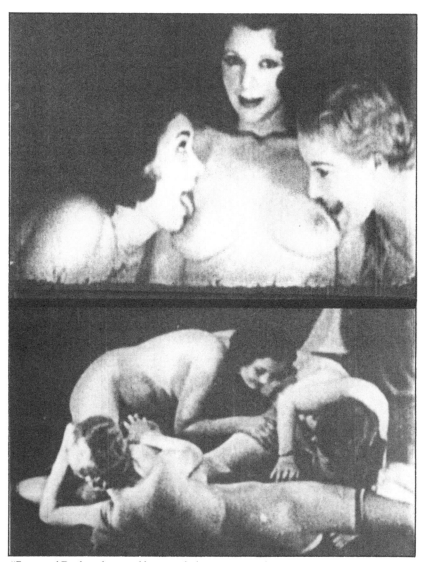

"Peggy and Dot have been paid honor with their tongues at the quivering cunnus of sweet Joan now prepare themselves to enjoy delightful debauches of secret cult."

Torture of Tickling Tongues, 1930-1935.

The girl is overjoyed and tests it out. An angel appears to admonish Santa, but he quickly removes her halo and wings and seduces her while the girl enthusiastically pedals away. The last shot shows Santa discreetly placing his mask over the girl's penetrated genitalia. The tone of the film suggests an amused tolerance and whimsicality infrequently seen in the stag film.

In *La Femme au Portrait* ("The Woman in the Portrait"), a couple purchases a portrait of a female flamenco dancer sitting under a mounted bull's head. The woman is drawn to the painting but the man has his mind on more carnal pleasures. After fucking the woman several times he chalks up his successes on the wall and dozes off. As the girl sits on the bed weeping, the dancer steps out of the painting and comforts her. The two women wake the man and force him into vigorous sexual activity, during which they erase his chalk marks. After exhausting him, the women fall asleep in each other's arms. When they awaken, the dancer leads the girl into the painting. The man wakes up just in time to see the women step in, but when he reaches the painting it is again two-dimensional. As he sits puzzling the bizarre events, the painting again comes to life; the dancer reaches up for the mounted bull's head and places it over the man's head like the horns of the classic cuckold. What is significant in the film, as in *Conte de Noël,* is the uncharacteristic emphasis on the female's sexual pleasure. *La Femme au Portrait,* with its turning of the tables and its denigration of male potency, is a far cry from the brutal *machismo* of the Latin American film.

The British film of the 1960s is of interest on several levels: it often involves settings more elaborate than the traditional stag, and it begins to stress "kinky" sexual behavior, sado-masochism, buggery, etc. Exterior shots of Hyde Park and Trafalgar Square place the films definitively, while several films (*What the Butler Saw, The Music Master, Incestral Home*) seem to have been shot in stately homes or expensively furnished flats. The *vices anglaises* of dominance, bondage, and sado-masochism, although usually not overt, are in evidence. Girls in school uniforms, masters, servants, governesses—the obsessive preoccupations of Victorian pornography—compete with modern salesgirls, airline stewardesses, as well as Soho tarts. Anal sex appears more frequently in films like *Rear Admiral,* as do themes of incest and paedophilia (sex with children), although the girls play younger than they actually are. The films show that the British pornographers know their audience's tastes quite well, for there is a particularly strong pattern of historical continuity in British pornography. The British blue film has largely been produced for an elite clientele drawn from the higher strata of society, unlike its American counterpart which remains, for the most part, defiantly plebian—as the frequently misspelled, often semi-literate, inter-titles reveal.

When pornography was legalized in Denmark in 1968 the result was a spate of visual pornography of a higher technical quality than any that had preceded it. Although energy was directed initially toward the publication of magazines—

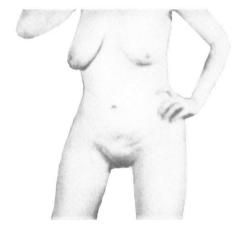

Torture of Tickling Tongues, 1930-1935.

Aunt Martha Visits Sadie, 1930's.

Color Climax, Color Orgasm, Weekend Sex, etc.—film production followed logically, with the same models. The films, intended for private viewing, remained within the short, small-gauge formula of contemporary stags, but being openly produced, they were now of professional quality, almost always in excellent color, occasionally with sound, and in multiple reels. As stigmas against appearing in such films eroded, the performers were almost uniformly young, attractive, and apparently amateurs. In recent years there has been a falling-off of quality due, no doubt, to increased international competition and local and tourist satiation. Perhaps for financial or distribution reasons, the Scandinavians did not develop the full-length pornographic feature despite a tradition of exploitation sex comedies like *Seventeen* ("Twice as good as 8½," one wag noted); the Americans were allowed to develop the porno and supply even the local public sex film market.

"My dearest sweetheart, who is fair and lovely, with her sweet and inspiring form she gives me thrills in life and that beautiful bust that I adore . . ."

Author's True Story, 1932-1936.

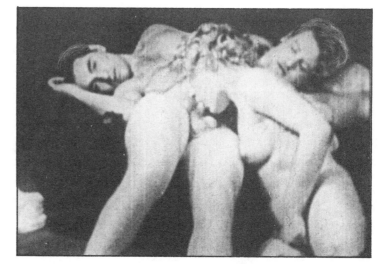

"A blond known as Trixie, A sepia gal named Carmen accept Bob Alcock's invite for a boat trip."

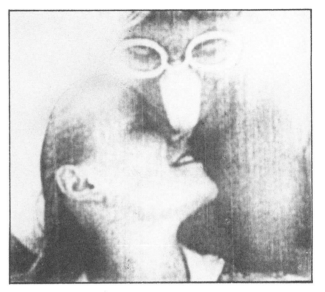

The narrative contents of the early Scandinavian films vary. Some contain non-stop sexual activity, though usually of an experimental nature. In contrast to the American stag in which the climax—esthetically and literally—traditionally consists of the man ejaculating on the female's belly (for the viewer's benefit), the Scandinavian coda invariably involves ejaculating on the woman's face or in her mouth (this has increasingly characterized the American, particularly New York, pornos). Other films were more ambitious. An Italian named Alberto Ferro, under the pseudonym of Lasse Braun, produced series of films with diverse historical and thematic emphases: a "tropical" series, apparently shot in the Caribbean, featuring black performers; a "prostitution" series about professional sex; an historical series devoted to the sexual adventures of Casanova (*Casanova and . . . the Country Girls, the Princess, the Nuns*); another series devoted to the sex-life of the Vikings; and three top-secret episodes from the adventures of Sex-Agent X-69. In recent years, he has increasingly focused on anal sex in *Deep Arse* and other series.

Trip to Pleasure Island, 1938.

Farmer's Daughter, 1930's.

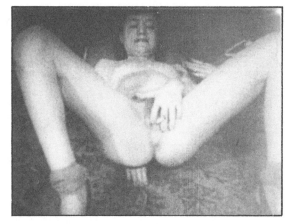

Aunt Martha Visits Sadie, 1930's.

Other film producers, such as Flesh Moving Pictures, Venus Films, and Color Climax Films, similarly began to offer thematically varied fare. Flesh offered such titles as *The Hangman's Night*, *The Perverted Dentist*, *Roman Orgy*, *The Potent Painter*, and *Witch's Sabbath*. Venus Films offered such series as Violence, Forbidden Variations (*The Negro and the Maid*, *Father and Daughter*), and Group Sex, and continued the sex humor tradition in *Even Thieves Do It* and *Sexy Clinic*. Color Climax preferred a more exclusive concentration on sexual activity. Its catalogue description—itself a species of literary pornography—of a film entitled *Sex Campus* (the universality of English titles indicates that the primary market was intended to be American or British) offers a typical example: "Twenty-one-year-old Ingrid has a permanent itch, a quivering pussy, a mouth always ready for a hot cock. As you will see she drains two men and afterwards masturbates herself. What a tigress." But another description cannot resist tongue-in-cheek parody: "This film portrays old fashioned simple sex. No sporty knots or acrobatics. A film for the over-sixties."

Among the exotica advertised in the Scandinavian catalogues is an interesting series of erotic animated cartoons, the provenance of which is unclear. The Venus catalogue illustrates three satiric pornographic versions of fairy tales which clearly seem to be the work of the same artist(s): two-reel versions of *Snow White the Cutie* and *Dornmöschen*, and a one-reel version of *Schwänzel and Gretel*. We have seen a print of the *Snow White* under the title *Schneeflittchen Hinter den Sieben Bergen* ("Snow White Behind the Seven Mountains"), which suggests that the entire series is of German origin. Yet Kyrou in his 1963 filmography notes *"une savoureuse satire de Blanche-Neige et les Sept Nains,"* which he unequivocally states is Italian. It is, of course, possible that he is referring to a completely different version, but *Schneeflittchen*, with its voluptuous heroine, its horny dwarfs, and its insatiable stepmother, surely fits Kyrou's description of a "tasty satire" of *Snow White*.

THEMES AND VARIATIONS

DESPITE NATIONAL DIFFERENCES, the stag film remained a consistent, rigidly defined form, esthetically limited by its brevity and method of production. Without the space/time of literary pornography it had to achieve its goals with great conciseness, recognizing that the more attention to dramatic embellishment, the less opportunity for its *raison d'être*, sexual activity. This formal brevity intensifies the universal theme that the stag shares with all pornography: the defenselessness of social, moral, and psychological restraints before the imperatives of lust. More than one pornographic heroine has admonished: "Stop talking and keep fucking." Or in the words of the slogan of the San Francisco *Ball:* "To ball is to live; everything else is just waiting." The mechanism for expressing the "Romance of Lust" in the stags is usually seduction of some kind, but since sex is invariably initiated with little or no resistance, the term is generous. Insofar as it tries to frame its sexual images dramatically, the stag sets up situations intended to trigger immediately lustful responses in its characters and hence in its audience. It collectively demonstrates that puritanic sanctions are foolish and hypocritical, that men and women are preeminently sexual animals. No age, class, or occupation is immune; in French films one observes the sexual comedy which en-

Blue Plate Special, 1940's.

91

snares dukes and duchesses, gamekeepers and laundresses, cooks and maids, painters and models, *modistes* and customers, and, of course, those who officially represent repressive, hypocritical morality, such as teachers, priests, and public officials.

American films, with their more particularly masculine focus, are less socially universal than the French; they range more widely through the spectrum of male occupations than female. Through the American films troop an army of handymen, milkmen, grocery boys, icemen, radio (and, later, television) repairmen, door-to-door salesmen, bill collectors, census takers, sex researchers, meter-readers, tramps, and burglars. These jobs have one thing in common— they bring the man into the home. These heroes of the American stag exist to respond to the overwhelming myth of the frustrated, lonely, horny housewife. More often than not it is she who makes the first move, at least by being sexually provocative. In postwar films, the "seduction" often takes place off-screen *before* the couple enters the hotel or motel room. The film can thus dismiss the preliminaries which restrict sexual footage.

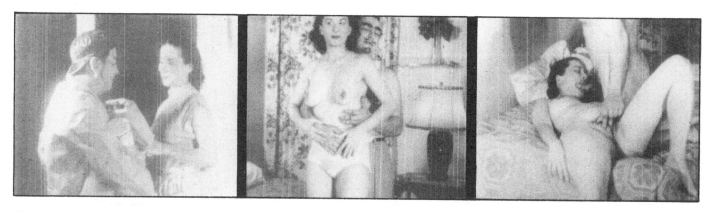

Black Market, 1948-52.

When the American stag heroine ventures out of the house she swiftly encounters sexual adventure, quite often in her doctor's office. It is significant how many American stags employ doctors as sexual predators: *Oh Doctor, Emergency Clinic, Lady Doctor, Doctor Long-peter, Doctor Penis, Doctor's Orders, Doctor Hardon's Injection, Doctor Fix'em, The Doctor's Prescription for Love*, and other such fictional and real practitioners as *Doctor Kildare, Calling Ben Casey*, and *Doctor Kinsey*, etc. Although there are several European doctor films, *Sexy Clinic* and *The Chiropodist* among them, they are not nearly as numerous as their American counterparts. This list attests to one of the obsessive fantasies in all pornography: the betrayal of professional trust in the name of sex. The doctor remains the American archetype of professional reverence. For the British it is usually the governess or teacher (master); for the Latins, the priest. Erotic tension, it would seem, particularly arises from the violation of relationships in which a participant is, by definition, trusting and vulnerable.

A corollary of this theme is the exploitation of power for sexual purposes, either through direct mind control—the hypnotist, the magician—or through

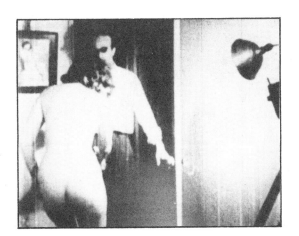

Blue Plate Special, 1940's.

93

Merry-Go-Round, 1947-1951.

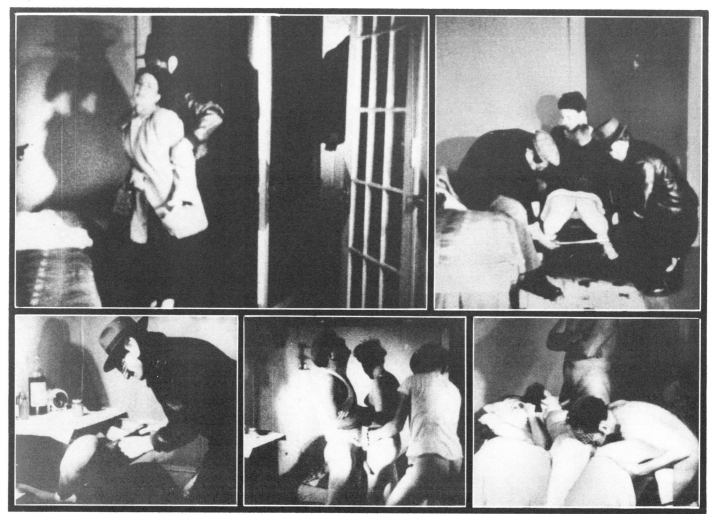

94

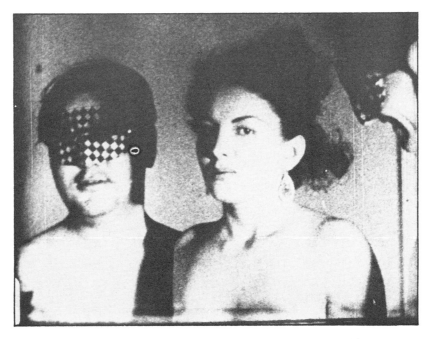

Merry-Go-Round, 1947-1951.

class and occupational dependencies—boss-secretary, master-servant, teacher-student, casting director-starlet. Lust is enhanced by social and psychic dominance; sexual advances are invariably at first resisted, then accepted and enjoyed by the socially weaker party, almost always—but not exclusively—the woman. (We have noted several films in which women turn the sexual tables and emerge dominant: *The Goat, La Femme au Portrait.*) In *The Casting Couch* (1924), for example, the standard seduction ends with the moral: "The only way to become a star is to get under a good director and work your way up."

95

Petit Conte de Noel, 1950.

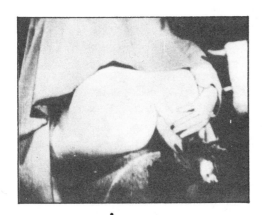

Transgression and dominance find extreme expression in themes of incest, paedophilia, and sado-masochism. Incest is the easiest of these taboos to depict because there is no way of knowing whether the performers are actually related. Film incest is no different from literary incest; it is a narrative convention. There are many films with incest themes: *Father's Daughter, Family Fun, Father Knows Best, Espirit de Famille, Family Affair, Mother's Daughter,* etc. Invariably, the "daughter" rarely appears to be much younger than the "parent." The other transgressions are different; the eye *should* provide its own verification. Indeed, paedophilia and sado-masochism are far less common in the classic stag film than in literary pornography, in which it is possible for the imagination to savor the idea of transgression without having to assimilate actual images of its realization. Although Latin-American films often include adolescent girls, true paedophiliac films (with pre-pubescent children) are almost non-existent, and many such still photographs exist. In the mid-1970s, however, as the peep arcades strive to remain ahead of the pornos in sexual audacity, films from India and Pakistan have surfaced with very young, obviously victimized children. In British films teenage girls are often dressed in schoolgirl uniforms to make them appear younger (a trend taken up by the American pornos to avoid the harsher legal sanctions against the exploitation of minors). During the twenties and thirties, however, few women in American stags were under twenty. This was probably due both to the availability of performers (largely from the world of professional vice) and to the middle-aged smoker crowd's aversion to watching girls the age of their daughters cavort sexually.

As for sado-masochism, it is extremely rare in the classic stag film. Few French films follow in the tradition of their countryman, the Divine Marquis; Kyrou's filmography lists but two: *Messe Noire* and *Le Manoir de Chatiment* ("The Manor of Punishment," 1948). Although S-M has always obsessed the British, the few examples of it one finds in their films are the softest of "soft fladge." And the few American stags we know of which treat the subject—as opposed to specialized (non-sexual to the non-initiate) bondage films—do not venture into the arcane, Gothic iconography of leather, whips, chains, and mechanical contrivances. Flagellation is uncommon—though women are struck—and bondage is clearly a prelude to genital sex. Psychic rather than physical domination is the goal. In *An English Tragedy*, based on a Victorian S-M novel, Alice's domination by the nefarious Jack leads quickly from bondage to conventional fucking. One of the few American stags with an S-M title, *Spanking Sadistic Love*, also contains as much conventional sex as sexual aggression (a bottle in the vagina).

Why then the mid-seventies proliferation of S-M material on all levels—hetero and homo, porno and peep? Sado-masochism's increasing command of

Petit Conte de Noel, 1950.

the mainstream pornography market undoubtedly represents an attempt (for commercial rather than esthetic reasons) to restore a sense of transgression and guilt to a genre weakened by toleration. When pornography was infused with the *frisson* of illegality, sado-masochism had a more specialized appeal.

Similarly, until the 1950s and 1960s we find few instances of anal sex (which some view as a variety of dominance). Analism becomes increasingly common as depicted sexual behavior moves away from the conventional. In the traditional American stag it is clearly a species of exotica: in *Playmates* (1950s) a light bulb inserted in a woman's anus tries to illuminate the mystery. For genuine anal fascination one must turn to the British (*Rear Admiral, Rear View*) and the Nordics (Scandinavians and Germans). Joseph Slade has pointed out, in *Society* magazine, that analism particularly obsesses countries with strong Protestant

Smart Aleck, 1951.

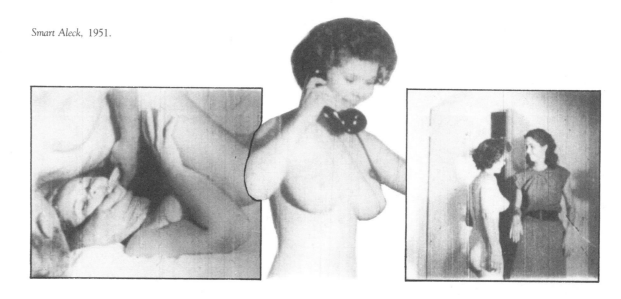

98

traditions. In the pornos' discovery of anal intercourse, America has shown its determination to make up for lost time.

One "perversion" which appears quite often in the traditional American stag is urolagnia, but not as one might expect in a male-dominated form, with the man urinating on the woman. Usually it is presented as a variation of the anatomy lesson—the woman urinates into a glass or other container. The act is often a form of homage to the mysterious female sexual apparatus. One is reminded of Mellors in *Lady Chatterley's Lover* marvelling that Connie's "Lady Jane" both makes love and pisses. In *The Farmer's Daughter* (1930s) female urine is used as an aphrodisiac. A girl is aroused by watching two horses mate. She urinates into a pail of drinking water and carries it to the hired hand in the field. After drinking it, he chases and catches her, and they have sex.

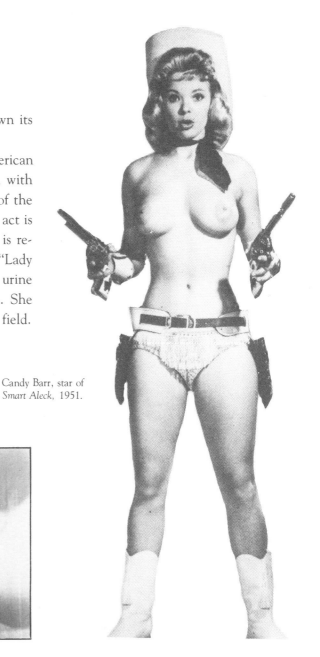

Candy Barr, star of
Smart Aleck, 1951.

99

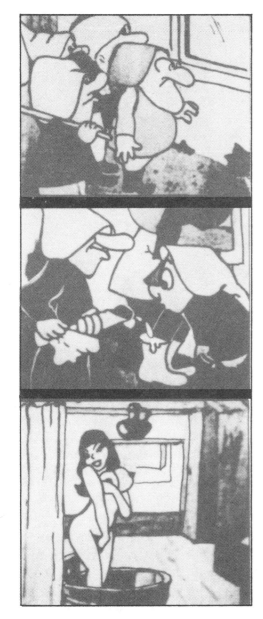

Snow White the Cutie, 1950's-1960's.

Snow White the Cutie, 1950's-1960's.

The stag film's reflection of evolving sexual values is instructive. Knight and Alpert estimate in their analysis of over one thousand stags from the 1920s through the 1960s—predominantly an American sample—that in over 50 percent of the films the cast consists of a single couple. In Kyrou's filmography the percentage is considerably less: 22 of 71 films feature a single couple, or 30.9 percent. As the American film moves toward the present, more instances of group sex with three, four, or more participants occur. In their sample Knight and Alpert also note a remarkable increase in oral-genital activity—both fellatio and cunnilingus: 37 percent of 1920s films include fellatio; in the 1930s the percentage increases to 48.5 percent and remains constant through the 1940s. In the 1950s, however, the figures leaps to 68 percent and then to 77.3 percent in the 1960s. At present oral-genital sex occurs in close to 100 percent of all pornos.

Cunnilingus, with its overtones of male subservience, is, as one might expect, much less common in the stag film. It appears in 11 percent of the films produced in the 1920s and in 12.6 percent of those made in the 1930s. But the radical increase in its depiction—16 percent in the 1940s, 32 percent in the 1950s, and 64 percent in the 1960s—reveals a major change in male sexual attitudes. The films reflect an increased toleration of sexual diversity. Even the strongest taboos have been severely challenged, if not demolished. In the 1920s white women and black males were paired in less than 1 percent of the films, while 6.8 percent of the decade's films paired a white man and a black woman. In the 1960s, however, the white male-black woman figure remains about the same, but the percentage of black man-white woman encounters increases to 4.4 percent. With the recent emergence of a large black urban market for the porno and the peep, the percentage of black-white contacts (advertised as "mixed combos") has increased radically.

The strongest taboo remains that against the depiction of male homosexuality, of which there are fewer examples in Knight and Alpert's sample than of bestiality (woman-dog films: 2.1 percent; exclusively male homosexuality: 1.4 percent). Occasionally, male homosexual contacts figured in otherwise heterosexual films—*A Stiff Game, Je Verbalise, The Chiropodist*—but for the stag audience, and particularly for the conservative American smoker crowd, such contact was particularly *verboten*. In the contemporary porno, by and large, the taboo holds; male homosexuality rarely appears in heterosexual films, much less frequently, for example, than even sado-masochism or "golden showers." Since the 1960s a distinctive gay genre has emerged which parallels the development of the pornographic film in general: through the stages of exploitation, "beaver," stag, to the currently flourishing gay porno. Before the 1960s, however, the gay audience was unorganized and fearful. One of the few early exclusively gay films to surface, *Three Comrades* (1950s), reveals an ambiguity as to which audience it

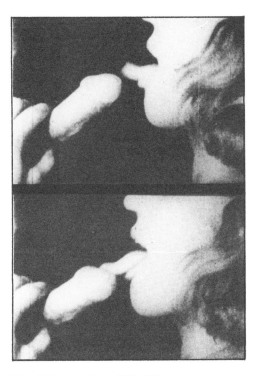

Hycock's Dancing School, 1932-1936.

was aimed. Consistent with the style of the 1950s, there is no dramatic context, just three men in an active homosexual threesome. The inter-titles, however, continue to comment in the familiar, earlier stag tradition: "As you will notice these fellows are all hung heavy from continually getting BLOWED OFF." The last inter-title is particularly puzzling; after a daisy-chain "Grand Finale" it comments: "Aw Shit. I'm Disgusted. So let us QUIT." One wonders if the film could have been intended (or adapted) for a straight audience as exotica, in the spirit of this title from another film: "You are now at a sideshow and will see the great freaks of passion perform." If the film were intended for a gay audience, why the expression of disgust?

Lesbian activity, on the other hand, is omnipresent in stag films of all countries in all periods (20 percent of Knight and Alpert's sample). In fact, this fascination with the sexual mysteries of the brothel, the convent, and the girls' school constitutes one of the primary erotic male fantasies. Why this male obses-

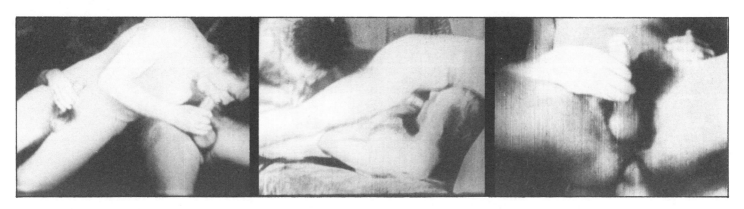

"As you will notice these fellows are all hung heavy from continually getting BLOWED OFF!"
Three Comrades, 1950-1960.

sion with lesbianism? Philip Wylie and Wayland Young have suggested that lesbianism offers the male fantasist two women for the price of one. Others suggest that its erotic power lies in the sense of transgression. Or, perhaps the attraction of lesbianism for male heterosexuals resides in the myth of the lustfully consumed, insatiable woman—the Devil in the Flesh—who is compelled to use anyone or anything (dogs, dildos, phallic substitutes, other women) to relieve her unrestrained sexual cravings (*The Devil in Miss Jones*, for example). By shifting the focus from the (supposedly) supererotic man to the lust-consumed woman who is able to satisfy herself without male aid if need be, men are partially relieved of the threatening virile role expected of them. In this regard, as Slade has acutely observed, filmed pornography is less anxiety-allaying than literary pornography. In literary pornotopia man is universally potent and inexhaustible; in the movies "frailty's name is man; he tires quickly and falls short of the multiple orgasms of his literary counterpart."

Mexican Dog, 1930's.

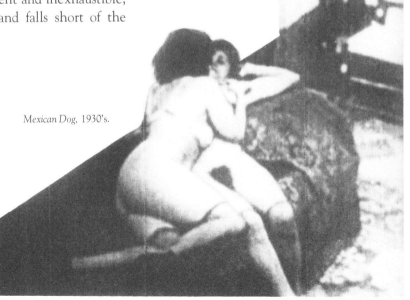

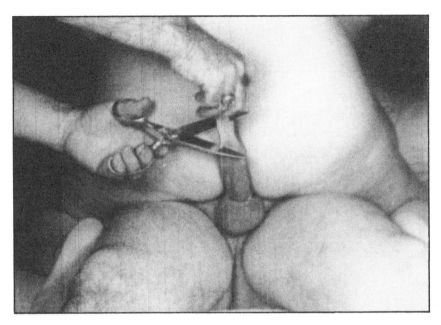

The Sexy Sexteens, part two, 1962-1963.

Male sexual anxiety is most urgently revealed by the castration theme in several films. In *Forever Limber* (1935-39) a girl comes upon a man chopping trees. They begin to have sex but the man is unable to get an erection. The frustrated girl sardonically decides he does not need his penis and picks up the ax to chop it off. And in *Sally and Her Boy Friend* (1948-52), when her boyfriend fails to recover from an initial sex bout fast enough to please her, Sally salts his penis, puts it between two slices of bread, and seemingly bites it off. Several pornos of the 1970s—including the first, *Electro-Sex* (1970)—as well as such serious films as Marco Ferreri's *The Last Woman* and Nagisa Oshima's *The Empire of the Senses* have similar dire conclusions. Obviously the nightmare on the dark side of male sexual fantasy is so vivid it must be exorcised.

END OF AN ERA

THE STAG ERA—if not the stag film itself—ended with the emergence of the publicly screened, hard-core film around 1970. As legal sanctions eroded, the nature of the production of pornographic materials changed drastically. For the first time large profits were to be made, and organized crime entered the field, principally in the exhibition and distribution areas. Yet despite the huge success of a few films such as *Deep Throat* and *Behind the Green Door*, the makers of and performers in pornographic films still share in few of the spoils. For most in the porno "industry," it remains a high-risk, low-profit enterprise.

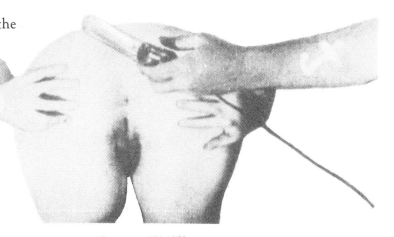

Playmates, 1956-1958.

That a direct line of continuity leads from the stags to the pornos is obvious. Despite the appearance of a few high-budget "quality" pornos such as *Wet Rainbow* and *Misty Beethoven*, the conditions for porno film making are not dissimilar from their clandestine predecessors: regional productions, stables of performers (particularly in New York production), hasty and cheap filming, maximum use of available footage. Plots are usually rudimentary excuses to initiate sexual action. This continuity can be clearly seen in *Little Sister*, an early porno (1971) which first screened the original stag version of *Espirit de Famille* (a French film of the late 1940s) and then recreated the action with contemporary performers. (In that film, as in some of the transitional pornos, actual and simulated penetration were combined.) Many later pornos rework traditional stag materials in much the same way.

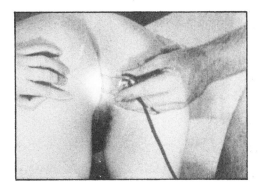

Although the porno has more time to fill than the stag—the standard length is an hour—the dramatic and thematic possibilities of this additional time have

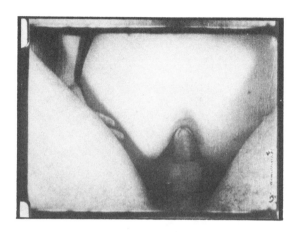

Playmates, 1956-58.

rarely been exploited. Basically, the porno has minimal dramatic structure; it usually depicts a series of sexual episodes designed so that each performer has about two sexual bouts. The porno equivalents of the purely sexual offerings of the 1940s-50s are the "loops," which contain no inner structure but present spliced, unrelated sexual encounters of about ten minutes' duration. One characteristic of the higher quality pornos from *Mona* through *Misty Beethoven* has been the esthetic recognition that the audience is not necessarily interested in numbers ("50 girls—count 'em—50"), but that the right heroine can sustain audi-

The Magician, 1930's.

ence involvement. Hence the appearance of porno "stars" like Linda Lovelace and Marilyn Chambers.

A few directors have attempted, with limited success, to develop the esthetic potential of the porno form. West-coast film makers such as Alex De Renzy (who helped surmount the last legal barriers), Bill Osco, the Mitchell Brothers, and Harry Hopper, after an initial outburst of creative energy resulting in a few imaginative films that suggested future possibilities, have been unable to demonstrate further growth. The porno director with the most substantial body of

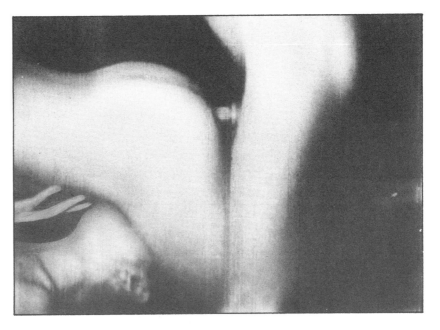

Three Comrades, 1950-1960.

The Pick-Up, 1923.

work is Gerard Damiano, who has attempted with mixed success to move the form toward traditional, open film making without sacrificing the erotic momentum of the genre. *Deep Throat,* building on the burlesque tradition of the early American stags, worked to sustain a farcical rhythm based upon the premise of a misplaced clitoris; *The Devil in Miss Jones* attempted to validate the myth of the lust-consumed woman by treating the serious theme of lust as the handmaiden of repression; *The Story of Joanna* took as its source the most successful of pornographic novels, *Histoire d'O.* Yet despite the increase of pornos of greater narrative and thematic complexity, the standard fare remains the episodic form of a series of unrelated sexual encounters. The stag is still the measure of the porno's esthetic reality.

The porno film, however, also has a non-clandestine source. It derives commercially from the exploitation film which through the decades has shown just the amount of sex with which it could legally escape. Unlike the stag, this

form is governed by hypocrisy. In the 1930s films such as *The Road to Ruin*, professionally made in sound and thirty-five-millimeter, exploited limited sexuality while endorsing public morality. This, of course, was a favorite strategy of the popular film of the Hollywood Production Code era: the taboo-breaking but sympathetic gangster or lawbreaker received official retribution in the final reel. After World War II the exploitation genre moved gingerly away from morality in a series of burlesque movies starring such well-known strippers as Tempest Storm and Lily St. Cyr.

In 1959 *The Immoral Mr. Teas* initiated a number of voyeuristic films in which sex itself was totally absent. In this genre a hapless, Milquetoast-type hero excited himself (and presumably the audience) by ogling fantasy images of nude women. *Mr. Teas* was made by Russ Meyer, who soon moved on to rougher terrain. In such films as *Motor Psycho*, *Lorna*, and *Faster Pussycat, Kill, Kill*, he combined a penchant for big-breasted voyeurism with brutal violence and melodrama. As restraints on language collapsed in the 1960s the exploitation film makers became bolder. When, under the guise of redeeming social value, the penetration barrier was finally broken by documentaries like *Censorship in Denmark* and *The History of the Blue Movie*, the exploitation film makers returned to the stags for materials and methods.

It might be thought that the public emergence of the porno would destroy—or at least severely retard—the private market traditionally serviced by

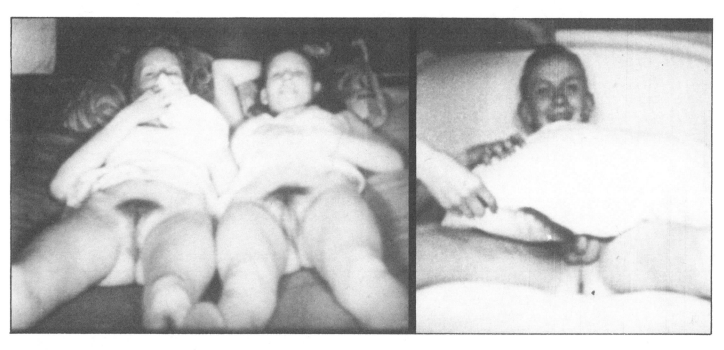

The Sexy Sexteens, part I, 1962-63.   *The Sexy Sexteens, part II, 1962-63.*

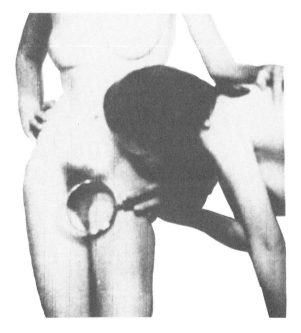

the illegal stag. The contrary has been true. The market has continued to expand. Called "private films," "mail orders," or "eights" (because the vast majority are eight- and supereight-millimeter shorts, usually the standard two-hundred feet in length), the stag film has benefited from the widening of the erotic market and continues to thrive. The films are no longer the exclusive preserve of fraternity men and legionnaires, no longer "stags" in an exclusively masculine sense. According to one distributor, one thousand new numbers are issued each year, produced largely in New York and California, and an increasing number of

The Sexy Sexteens, part II, 1962-63. 111

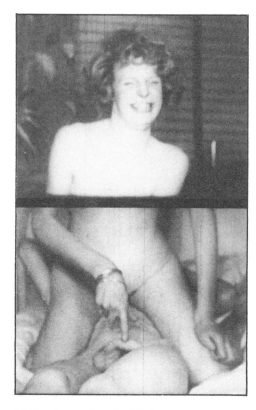

The Sexy Sexteens, Part II, 1962-63.

European films have surfaced on the American market. The current eights are usually of professional technical quality, in color, invariably silent, and often present the star performers of the pornos. (Two popular eight series feature the pre-*Throat* films of Linda Lovelace and the thirteen-inch penis of the ubiquitous superstar John C. Holmes.)

One result of the proliferation of this new material has been the accelerated disappearance of the older stag material from the private market. For almost half a century the haphazard, limited nature of stag distribution resulting from its illegality had created a situation in which the older films, duped and reduped, maintained their marketability. With the technically higher quality contemporary material now available, the faded black-and-white images of the past are losing their erotic power. The films illustrated in this book are an endangered species.

The new American eights are dramatically less inventive than their Scandinavian (and German and Dutch) counterparts, though there is some use of

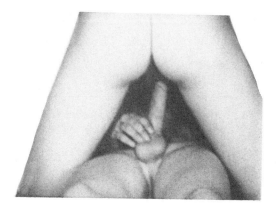

The Sexy Sexteens, part I, 1962-63.

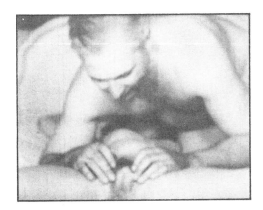

The Sexy Sexteens, part II, 1962-63.

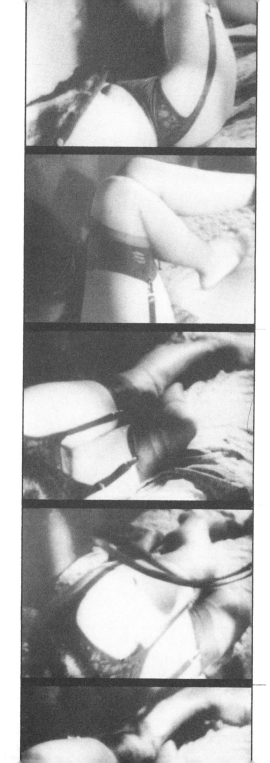

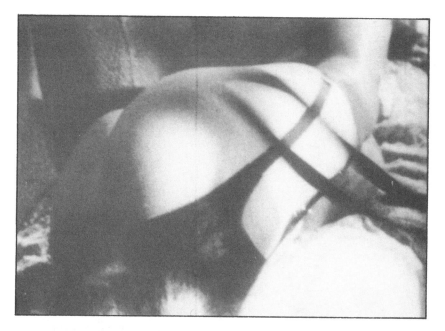

Spanking Sadistic Love, 1966

exterior shooting and rudimentary plot. The form is largely determined by the ways the films are to be marketed. Although most are sold across- or under-the-counter in sex bookstores or through the mail, much of their revenue derives from their display in peep-show arcades, often in the back of these shops. The peep show returns the film to its penny-arcade origins. *What the Butler Saw* (very little) enticed generations of males to the arcades of Coney Island and elsewhere. The public peeps showed the palest of erotica, their titles being the most daring thing about them. By the 1950s they became bolder, and gradually, as local

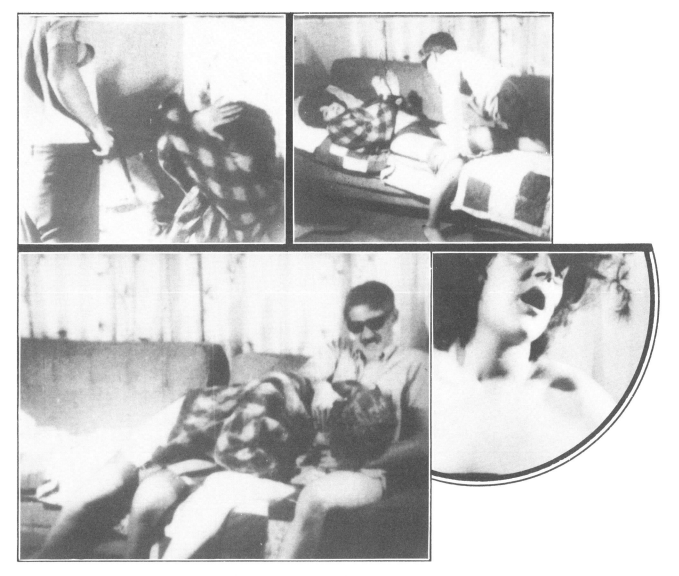

Spanking Sadistic Love, 1966.

In The Name of Odin, 1970.

pressures warranted, they became more explicitly sexual. By the mid-1970s they were more perverse than the pornos in the attempt to provide the viewer with more potent, transgressing images than those available publicly.

Changes in the architecture of the viewing area have aided this trend. Some clever entrepreneur, recognizing the limitations of side-by-side viewing, decided to create, through curtains and machine placement, private cubicles in his arcade. This isolated the viewer and facilitated masturbation. The first example with which we are familiar was in Chicago in the early 1950s. With the proliferation of peep shows in the sex strips of major cities, the cubicles have become in the fancier emporia private chambers which offer a multiple choice of films. A ten-minute film is usually divided into five segments of two minutes each, each section triggered by a quarter. Since the film remains at the part of the film abandoned by the previous viewer, a new quarter might begin a sequence from the middle or end of the film. Obviously, in such circumstances plot and narrative become irrelevant.

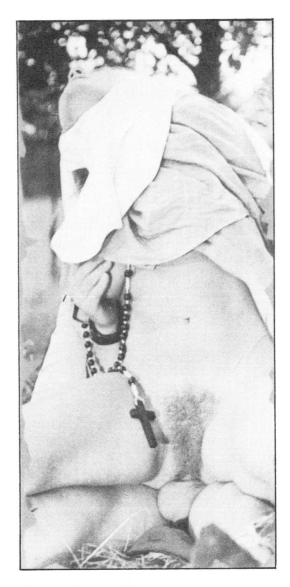

Victory For The Queen, 1970.

117

THE STAG IS DEAD, long live the stag. Despite some weakening of the genre through its public surfacing, the stag film and its variants, it seems, are not about to disappear. Perhaps as open art, if unsuppressed, increasingly responds to sexual imperatives, the pornographic vision will have outlived its usefulness. Or perhaps the public/private schism in our culture is too deep to heal. We have created a world in which, paradoxically, the fear of sexuality has constructed an obsessive monument to sex itself. In documenting the dramas of our mythic and fantasy lives, the stag film has shown us as the sexual animals we fear to be. It affirms a liberating anarchy we are terrified might destroy our social institutions. Its dogged survival, despite severe prohibitions, makes it a matter of social and psychological importance. If its single-mindedness represents an imbalance between body and spirit, the pornographic vision may be seen as a symptom of disorder rather than a cause. But for its affirmation of the pleasures of the body without the weight of social consequences, for its open acceptance of our common human needs, we can be grateful. In entering pornotopia it is comforting to forget for awhile that man does not live by head alone.

BIBLIOGRAPHY

The literature *on* pornography exceeds the literature *of* pornography. The following bibliography, then, is inevitably selective, particularly regarding periodical entries. It is intended (1) to indicate the sources upon which the text of this book is based; and (2) to provide a basic list of significant works on various aspects of the subject.

I. PORNOGRAPHY, OBSCENITY, AND THE LAW

Chandos, John, ed. *To Deprave and Corrupt.* London: Souvenir Press, 1962.

Craig, Alec. *The Banned Books of England.* London: George Allen and Unwin, 1962.

Ernst, Morris L., and Seagle, William. *To the Pure. . .* New York: Viking Press, 1928.

Gagnon, John H., and Simon, William. "Pornography—Raging Menace or Paper Tiger?" *Trans-Action,* July/August 1967, pp. 41-48.

Kronhausen, Eberhard and Phyllis. *Pornography and the Law.* New York: Ballantine Books, 1959.

Lawrence, D. H. *Sex, Literature, and Censorship.* New York: Viking Press, 1953.

"The Porno Plague." *Time,* April 5, 1976, pp. 58-63.

Rembar, Charles. *The End of Obscenity.* New York: Random House, 1968.

The Report of the Commission on Obscenity and Pornography. New York: Bantam Books, 1970.

Rolph, C. H., ed. *Does Pornography Matter?* London: Routledge and Kegan Paul, 1961.

————. *The Trial of Lady Chatterley.* London/New York: Penguin Books, 1961.

St. John-Stevas, Norman. *Obscenity and the Law.* London: Secker and Warburg, 1956.

Scott, George Ryley. *Into Whose Hands.* London: Gerald G. Swan, 1945.

Steiner, George. "Night Words." *Language and Silence.* New York: Atheneum Publishers, 1967.

II. PORNOGRAPHY, ART, AND SOCIETY

Ashbee, Henry Spencer. *A Complete Guide to Forbidden Books.* New York: Brandon House, 1966.

Buchen, Henry, ed. *The Perverse Imagination: Sexuality and Literary Culture,* New York: New York University Press, 1970.

Conrad, Peter. "Potent Images." *Times Literary Supplement,* February 20, 1976, pp. 190-91.

Dury, David. "Sex Goes Public: A Talk with Henry Miller." *Esquire,* May 1966, pp. 118-21, 170-71.

Elsom, John. *Erotic Theatre.* New York: Delta Books, 1975.

Foxon, David. *Libertine Literature in England, 1660-1745.* New Hyde Park, N.Y.: University Books, 1965.

Gorer, Geoffrey. *The Life and Ideas of the Marquis de Sade.* New York: W. W. Norton and Co., 1962.

Legman, Gershon. *The Rationale of the Dirty Joke. First Series.* New York: Castle Books, 1968.

Loth, David. *The Erotic in Literature.* New York: Julian Messner, 1961.

Marcus, Steven. *The Other Victorians.* New York: Basic Books, 1966.

Melville, Robert. *Erotic Art of the West.* London: Weidenfeld and Nicolson, 1974.

Michelson, Peter. *The Aesthetics of Pornography.* New York: Herder and Herder, 1971.

"Obscenity in Folklore." *Journal of American Folklore*, July/September 1962.

Peckham, Morse. *Art and Pornography.* New York: Harper and Row, 1969.

Rawson, Philip. *Erotic Art of the East.* New York: G. P. Putnam's Sons, 1968.

Sontag, Susan. "The Pornographic Imagination." *Styles of Radical Will.* New York: Delta Books, 1969.

Vidal, Gore. "On Pornography." *New York Review of Books*, March 31, 1966, pp. 4-9.

Young, Wayland. *Eros Denied.* New York: Grove Press, 1966.

III. PORNOGRAPHY, EROTICISM, AND FILM

Barr, Candy. "Interview." *Oui*, June 1976, pp. 81-84, 110-13.

Blake, Roger. *The Porno Movies.* Cleveland: Century Books, 1970.

Durgnat, Raymond. *Eros in the Cinema.* London: Calders and Boyars, 1966.

Hoffmann, Frank. *Analytical Survey of Anglo-American Traditional Erotica.* Bowling Green, Oh.: Bowling Green University Popular Press, 1973.

_____. "Prolegomena to a Study of Traditional Elements in the Erotic Film." *Journal of American Folklore*, April/June 1965, pp. 143-48.

Knight, Arthur, and Alpert, Hollis. "The History of Sex in Cinema." *Playboy*, 19 articles published from April 1965 to January 1969.

_____. "The Stag Film," *Playboy*, November 1967, pp. 154-58, 170-89.

Kyrou, Ado. *Amour, Erotisme au Cinéma.* Paris: La Terrain Vague, 1957.

_____. "D'un Certain Cinema Clandestin."
Positif: Revue de Cinéma, combined nos. 61, 62, 62, June/July/August 1964, pp. 205-23. (Combined issue devoted to eroticism in film.)

Lo Duca. *L'Erotisme au Cinéma.* vols. I-III. Paris: Pauvert, 1958, 1960, 1962.

Martin, Olga J. *Hollywood's Movie Commandments.* New York: H. W. Wilson, 1937.

Moley, Raymond. *The Hays Office.* New York and Indianapolis: Bobbs-Merrill Co., 1945.

Slade, Joseph. "Pornographic Theatres off Times Square." *Trans-Action.* November/December 1971, pp. 35-43, 79.

_____. "Recent Trends in Pornographic Films." *Society* (formerly Transaction), September/October 1975 pp. 77-84

Turan, Kenneth, and Zito, Stephen F. *Sinema.* New York: Praeger Publishers, 1974.

Tyler, Parker. *Screening the Sexes.* New York: Holt, Rinehart and Winston, 1972.

_____. *Sex, Psyche, Etcetera in the Film.* New York: Horizon Press Publishers, 1969.

Vogel, Amos. *Film as a Subversive Art.* New York: Random House, 1974.

Walker, Alexander. *The Celluloid Sacrifice.* London: Michael Joseph, 1966.

FILMOGRAPHY AND TITLE INDEX

This alphabetical listing of stag films does not include all known extant stag materials (there are over 1200 entries in the Institute for Sex Research film catalogue alone). It aims, rather, to serve as a reference for films cited in the text and to provide a sense of the sweep of 60 years of international stag film making. The list derives from several sources: (1) films seen by the authors in the United States and abroad; (2) significant titles from the ISR collection; (3) Ado Kyrou's invaluable *Positif* filmography; (4) films from Scandinavian catalogues of the late 1960s, early 1970s; and (5) the catalogue listings of one of the United States' most extensive private stag collections (the owner of which must remain anonymous), provided by our very own "Deep Throat."

Given the illegal, fugitive nature of the genre, the dating of these films is a tricky business. In some cases we have redated films on the basis of new evidence; in others, we have accepted the authority of our sources. In only one instance we know of does a film date itself; *Wonders of the Unseen World*, parodying open movie credits, claims in its main titles to be "copyrighted 1927," and evidence suggests the legitimacy of this date. A few films offer definitive evidence in the form of literary allusions. *Hot Party* begins with the inter-title: "The girls who are fugitives from the Grand Hotel decide that Strange Interlude at their apartment is like a lot of Laughter in Hell with a Silver Dollar." The book/play title references clearly place the film in the early 1930s. For the most part, however, the dating of films depends upon external evidence, such as when the film first appeared on the stag market, and internal evidence which identifies the period reflected in the film's images and technique—clothes, coiffeurs, cars, decor, bawdy titles, the number of set-ups, use of zoom lenses, and so on.

KEY TO THE LISTINGS

Parentheses around a title indicate the film's alternate title(s). Refer to accompanying title in the list.

(A), (B), (C), etc., after a title distinguish different films with the same titles.

(V-1) or (V-2) after a title indicates different versions edited from an original film.

Unless otherwise noted, the listed film originated in the United States.

Abbreviations:

M-Male F-Female   O-Oriental B-Black
L-Latin American X-Masked or Disguised
Y-Unusually young   A-Unusually aged
Z-Animal

A Bicyclette —2M, F, France, 1933

Accidental Lover —M, F, 1950s

Accidente Afortunado, Un —3LF, Cuba, 1949-52

(Adios) —Man and Wife (Part I)

(Adoree) —Young Couple (A)

Adventure —2M, F, 1958-62

Adventures Abroad —3F, 1930s

Adventures of Christina —M, F, 1920-26

Adventures of Pete the Tramp, The —Fat M, F, 1949-55

Ad-Vice —2M, F, England, 1968

African Intruder —BM, F, England, 1960-65

After School —M, 2F, England, 1966-67

After School Earnings —M, F, England, 1963-66

(After Six) —For After Sex

After the Ball —M, F, 1930s

After the Masquerade Ball (Parts I and II) — XM, XF, 1953

After the Party —M, 2F, England, 1968

(Air Conditioner Repairman) —Plumber's Son

A la Cuisine —M, F, France (Dominique), 1922

A l'Ecu d'Or —2M, 2F, France, 1908

Algerienne, L' —M, F, France, Germany, 1937

All Action —M, F, England, 1968

Allan and Laura Have a Ball —LM, LF, F, 1967

(All Fed Up) —All Fucked Up

(All Fouled Up) —All Fucked Up

All Fucked Up —M, F, 1965-66

All in Black —2M, 2BF, England, 1967-68

Amies, Les —2F, 1950-55

(Amies Girls, Les) —Amies, Les

Amorous Lesbians —M, BF, F, England, 1966

Ancient Rome 1968 —M, 2BM, 3F, 1967

Anniversary Party —M, BF, 1949-52

Announcer, The —M, F, 1966

Anxious Maiden Gets Relief —2M, 2F, 1948-52

(Anybody's Apartment) —Super Salesman

Anything Goes (A) —XM, F, BF

Anything Goes (B) —2M, 2F, England, 1967

Apartment —2YM, Sweden, 1960s

Apéritif Bien Servi, Un —3M, F, France (Nathan), 1920

Après la Classe —M, 3F, France (Dominique), 1925

Après le Bain —M, F, Spain, 1935

(Arabian, The) —After the Masquerade Ball

(Around the World) —Threesome, The (A)

(Art Collector) —Mortimer the Salesman

Artist, The —Fat M, F, 1950-55

Artist and I, The —M, F, 1967

Artist Model —M, F, 1946-50

Artists and Models —2M, 2F, 1958-63

(Artist's Model) (A) —Artist Model

(Artist's Model) (C) —Artist, The

(Art of Fucking, The) —One Dark Knight

Art of Love, The —M, F, 1930s

Assassinat de la Mendiante, L' —M, F, France, 1937

126

(At Home) —Evening at Home, An (B)
Atomic Jazzer —2M, YF, 1946-51
Aunt Martha Visits Sadie —2F, 1930s
Au Pair Rape —M, 2F, England, 1965-66
Author's True Story —2M, F, 1932-36
(Automatic Butt) —Three Pals
Auto Sapho [sic]—2F, England, 1965-66
Auto Sex—M, F, England, 1968
Avec Ses Pieds —M, F, France, 1946

Baby Doll —M, F, England, 1966-67
Baby Sitter (A) —M, F, 1947-49
Baby Sitter (B) —XM, XBF, 1948-55
(Baby Sitter Troubles) —Baby Sitter (B)
Bachelor and the Maid, The —M, F, 1950-56
(Bachelor Apartment) —Picolo [sic] Pete
Bachelor Girl Has Her Problems (Part II) —M, F, 1958-62
Bachelor's Dream —M, F, 1952-54
(Bad Dreams) —Nightmare (B)
Baignade, La —M, F, France, 1930
Ball 'n' Baby —M, F, 1968
(Banana Split) —Jane's Masseur
Banana Split —2M, F, England, 1966-67
Bang —M, F, 1965-67
(Bang Up Party) —Young Movement
Barbara (A) —M, F
Bare Interlude, A —M, F, 1928-33
Barker, The —2M, F
(Bartender, The) —Entre Dos Fuegos
(Bashful Bo) —Twelve Different Ways
(Bashful Fisherman) —Fisher Woman
(Bath) —Bath Room Scene

Bathing Susannah, The —2M, 2F, Denmark, 1970
(Bathroom, The) —Bathroom Frolics
Bathroom Frolics —2M, F, 1949-52
Bath Room Scene —2XYM, XYF, 1966
Bathroom Whims —M, F, 1958-62
Bat Man (A) —2M, F, 1964-66
Batman (A) —2M, F, 1966
Batman (B) (Part II) —2M, 2F, 1966-67
Beach Buggery —M, 2F, England, 1967-69
Beach Girl (A) —M, F, 1955-65
Beach Girls —3F, Denmark, 1969
Bearded Vibrator —M, F, 1966
Beat Generation (Parts I and II) —M, F, 1964-66
Beatles, The —M, F, 1965-66
Beat Me Daddy —M, F, 1930s
Beatnick Bedlam (Parts I and II) —M, F, England, 1966
(Beatnick Love) —Beat Generation (Part II)
Beau Champignon, Le —M, F, France (Nathan), 1924
Beauty —M, 2F, 1939-41
Beauty and the Beast —M, F, England, 1968
Beauty and the Boxer —F, Z, 1956
(Beaver Shot) —Errand Boy
(Beck and Call) —Valentino (V-2)
Bed Geisha —M, 2F, Denmark, 1969
Bed Party —M, 2F, 1967
(Bedroom Frolics) —Threesome, The (A)
Bed Session —M, F, England, 1965-67
Bedside Temptation —M, 2F, 1936-39
Bed Time —M, F, 1965-66

127

(Bellboy, The) —Bellboy 19
Bellboy 19 —M, F, 1930-35
(Bellhop, The) —The Intruder
(Ben Casey) (Parts I and II) —Calling Ben
   Casey (Parts I and II)
Bends, The —2M, 2F, 1958-62
Be Prepared —M, F, England, 1966-67
Beyond the Sunset —M, F, England, 1965-67
Big and Long —M, BF, 1960-63
Big and White —M, F, 1960-63
(Big Bad Bill) —Rod Rammer
(Big Bad Wolf and Two Little Red Hoods That
   Rode) —Wolfman (Parts I and II)
(Big Blow) —My Hero
(Big Boy) —Mexican Big Dick
(Big Business) —Good Mixers
Big Daddy —M, BF
(Big Dealer) —Fat Man
Big Event, The (A) —2M, F, 1945-50
(Big Event) (B) —One Hot Night
(Big Payoff) —Gigolo, The (A)
Big Sister —M, 2F, 1965-66
Big Surprise —2M, 2F, Denmark, 1970
Big Tits (A) —M, F, 1964-66
Bill Collector —2M, 2F, 1947-51
Bi-Sexuals —2M, 2F, England, 1967
Bisexual Buggery —M, 2F, England, 1968-70
Bits and Pieces —2M, F, 1958-62
(Black and White) (A) —Anniversary Party
Black and White (B) —BM, F, 1967
Black and White Fantasy —BM, M, BF, F,
   1949-53
Black and White Frolics —BM, 2F, England,
   1966-67

(Black Angus) —Two Nights and a Day (V-1)
Black Beast —BM, M, F, England, 1968
Black Bubbles —BM, F, England, 1964-67
(Black Hose) —Take My Daughter!
Black Mac —M, 2F, England, 1966-67
Blackmail —M, 2F, England, 1966
Black Market —M, F, 1948-52
Black Mass —XM, 10F, Germany 1920s
Black Power —2BM, F, England, 1968-70
Black Triangle —M, BF, F, Denmark, 1970
(Blanket Ideas) —Honeymoon Cottage
Blends —M, BF
Blimp, The —M, F, 1966
(Blonde Bonnet) —Fireside Lights
Blonde Hitch Hiker —M, F, 1955-56
(Blondie) (A) —Matinee Idol
(Blondie) (B) —Free Lunch
(Blondie and Her Friends) —Modern Art of
   Love
(Blondie and Her Pals) —Three Pals
(Blondie Blondell) —Matinee Idol
(Blondie Makes Good) —Motel Moderne
   (V-1)
Bloney Salesman —M, BF, 1966
(Blood Hound, The) —Brown Bomber
Blow Job, The —XM, F, 1955-65
Blows for Mr. Charlie —M, BF
(Bluebelle) —English Joys
Blue Denim —YM, YF, 1960-65
Blue Plate Special (V-1) —2M, 3F, 1940s
Blue Plate Special (V-2) —2M, 3F, 1940s
Boarder, The —M, F, 1958-62
(Bohemian, The) —Bohemio, El
Bohemio, El —LM, LF, Mexico, 1930s

Bondage —M, F, England, 1967

Bone Ass, The —M, F, 1949-53

Bonnie and Clyde —M, F, 1968-70

(Boogie Colored Girls) —Rum Boogie

(Boogie Woogie) —Rum Boogie

Book —M, BF, 1962-65

Bookie (A) —M, F, 1958-63

Bookie (B) —M, F, 1966

Book Worm —M, F, Germany, 1960-62

Boom Boom Jim —M, F, 1958-62

Bordello, The —M, F, Denmark, 1969-70

(Bottle Babes) —Caught By Surprise (Part II)

Bottle Me Darling —2M, F, England, 1966-67

Boxer Dog —F, Z, 1950-55

Boyfriend (A) —2M, XBF, 1964-66

Boyfriend (B) —M, F, 1958-63

Boy Fun —3YM, 1968

Boy Oh Boy (Parts I, II, and III) —6M, 1965-66

Boys, The —2M, 1959-62

(Boy's Party) —Browning Version

Boy Wanted —M, 3F, 1968-70

(Bra and Panties) —Late Date

Breaking in Blondie —M, 2F, 1947-48

Bridge Game —2M, 2F, 1967-69

(Bring Your Tool) —Handyman, The (A)

Broadway Interlude —2M, 2F, 1931-33

(Brother John) —Cheater (Part 1)

Brown Bomber —2M, F, Z, 1956

Browning Version —6M, 1968

(Bucket Brigade) —Talk of the Town

(Bug Juice) —Unexpected Company (A) (Parts 1 and 11)

(Bugs Bunny) (Parts I and II)—Unexpected Company (A) (Parts I and II)

Bum Fun —M, 2F, England, 1967-68

Bungalow Capers —2F, 1965

Burglar Boy —M, F, 1948-52

Burglar Makes a Deal, The —M, F, 1945-50

Buried Treasure —animated cartoon, 1928-33

Burlesque Queen —Fat M, F, 1949-55

Busty —LM, LF, Cuba, 1948-55

Busy Girl —M, F, 1939-44

Busy Lesbian Club —3F, 1930s

Butcher Boy —2M, 2F, 1950-55

Cabinet du Dr. Caligary [sic] —M, 2F, France, 1947-50

Cabinet Particulier —3M, 2F, Austria, 1928

(Caller, The) —Cheater (Part II)

Call For Dr. Handsome —M, F, 1948-55

(Call Girl) (A) —Cover Girl

Call Girl (B) —BM, F, 1964

Call Girl (C) —M, F, 1963-66

Call Girl (D) —M, F, 1968-70

Call Girl, The (E) —2M, F, Denmark, 1969-70

Calling Ben Casey (Parts I and II) —M, F, 1965-66

Call WA 9-3782 —M, F, 1968

(Camear [sic] Man, The) —Camera Man, The

Camera Bug —M, F, 1960-62

Camera Man, The —2M, F, 1958-62

Camping Frauden —M, F, Germany, 1964-66

Canard, Le —2M, F, duck, France, 1926
Candid Camera —M, F, 1966
Candle and Whips —M, 3F, 1968
Candy —2F, 1966-67
(Candy Barr) —Smart Aleck (V-1)
Canotage —M, F, France, 1942
Captive —M, F, England, 1965-67
(Cartoon) —Buried Treasure
Casting Couch —M, F, 1924
(Casting Director, The) —Casting Couch
Castro (Part I) —M, F, 1965-66
Castro (Part II) —M, 2F, 1965-66
Cat Burglar (A) —XM, F, 1967
Cat Burglar (B) —M, 2F, England, 1964-66
Cat Girl —BM, F, 1967-69
(Cathy) —Paying the Bills
Caught! —M, BF, F, England, 1966-67
Caught by Surprise (Parts I and II) —BF, F, 1964-66
Caught in the Act (A) —M, F, 1964-66
Caught in the Act (B) —M, 2F, 1966
Caught in the Act (C) —M, 2F, England, 1967
(C. Banana) —Who Is Mary Poppin'?
Census Taker —M, F, 1946-50
(Central Park) —Young Couple,
(Chaise Lounge Affair, The) —Dream Job
Chance Inesperado, Un —M, F, pre-Castro Cuba
Change of Plans —M, BF, 1964-66
Change Partners —2M, F, 1965-66
Changing Partners —M, 2F, 1950-55
(Chastity Belt) —The Locksmith
Cheater (Part I) —MB, F, 1940s

Cheater (Part II) —2BM, F, 1940s
Checker Players —BM, M, BF, F, 1966
(Checkers) —Chess
Cherrys Galore —2M, 2F, 1968
Chess —M, F, 1961-62
Chez le Docteur —M, 2F, France, 1930
Chez le Peintre —M, 2F, Austria, 1927
China Doll —M, OF, 1959-62
China Girl —M, OF, 1960-65
(China Love) —Chinese Love Life
(Chinese Babe) —China Doll
(Chinese Delivery Boy) —Black Market
Chinese Love Life —M, 2OF, 1920s
(Chinese Man) —Black Market
(Chiropodist, The) (V-1) —Untouchable, The
Chiropodist, The (V-2) —2M, F, France 1920s
Choice Stuff —M, F, 1967
(Christina) —Adventures of Christina
(Christmas Cheer) —Tree, The
Christmas Dream —XM, F, 1940s
(Circus) —Burlesque Queen
(Clam Bake) —Burglar Boy
(Clean Break) —Burglar Boy
Clean-Cut Truck Driver —M, F, 1964-66
Clean Floors —2M, F, 1958-63
Cleaning Woman, The —M, BF, 1960-65
Clean Shave —M, F, Germany, 1960-63
Closely Related —M, F, England, 1965-66
(Close Shave) —A Bare Interlude
(Closet) —While the Cat's Away
(Clown) —Burlesque Queen
Club X —group, Denmark, 1968-70
Cockeyed Porter —M, F, 1947-48

Cock Sucker—2M, 1965-67
Cocktail à Trois—M, 2F, Italy, 1949
Cock Tails—M, 2F
(Coeds in School)—Night School (Part II)
(Coffee Break) (A)—Coffee Regular
Coffee Break (B)—2M, 1965-67
Coffee Regular—M, BF, 1965-66
Coiffeur, Le—M, F, France (Dominique), 1926
Cokie—M, F, 1947-51
(College Coed)—Nun's Story, The
College Tuition a Go-Go—M, F, 1964-66
Colored Rainbow—M, F, England, 1964-66
Combing Around—M, F, 1960-65
Come Alive—M, F, 1968-70
Come and Get It (A)—M, F, 1965-67
Come and Get It (B)—M, F, 1960-67
Comedy of Errors—2M, F, 1962-64
Come Fuck with Me—2F, 1968
(Comic Book Blondie)—Superman (B)
(Coming Attraction)—Natural Break, A
Coming Out—M, BM, F
Como Quiere un Mexicano—3M, F, Mexico, 1935-39
Companions, The—2M, 1968-70
Confidential Circus—M, 2F, 1930-35
(Conte de Noël)—Petit Conte de Noël
Cool Cats (Parts I and II)—M, 2F, 1966-67
Cop Cops, The—M, 2BM, 2F, 1967
Corruption (Part I)—M, 2F, England, 1968
Costly—M, F, 1966-67
(Cottage Capers)—Bungalow Capers
(Count Comes Home)—Gay Count, The
Country Cousin (A)—XM, XF, 1962-64

Country Cousin (B) (Parts I and II)—2M, 3F, 1967
(Country Doctor)—Dr. Longpeter
Country Girls (B)—2F, England, 1966-67
Country Watcher (Parts I and II)—2M, F, England, 1966-67
Cover Girl—M, F, 1948-55
Crazy Cat House—M, 2F, 1930s
Crazy Time—2XYM, XYF, 1966
Crib Time—M, F, 1964-66
Cri de la Chair, Le—M, 2F, Germany, 1952-53
(Crime Does Not Pay)—Escape (V-2)
Crowded Bed—M, 2F, 1968
Cuban Dream—LM, LF, Pre-Castro Cuba
Cuban Interlude—3M, 2F, Cuba, 1935-45
Cueillette des Olives, Le—M, 2F, France, 1930
Cum [sic] Clean—M, F, England, 1968
Cuntry [sic] Girls (A)—M, 2F, England, 1964-66
(Cuntry [sic] Girls) (B)—Country Girls (B)

Daily Duty—M, F, 1950-55
Daisy—M, F, 1966
(Daisy Chain)—Fiesta
(Dama de Negro, La)—Rin-Tin-Tin Mexicano
Dancer, The—LM, LF, 1964-65
Dancer's Interlude (V-1)—2M, BF, 1945-50
Dancer's Interlude (V-2)—2M, BF, 1945-50
Dancing Pal (Parts I and II)—2M, 3F, 1967
Dancing Party—M, F, 1966

Dancing Teacher, The (A) —M, F, 1935
Dancing Teacher (B) —M, F, England, 1966
Dancing Teacher (C) —M, F, 1968
(Dangerous Dan McGrew —Dancer's Interlude (V-2)
Darkie Rhythm —BM, BF, 1932-35
(Dark Love) —Inez
(Darling Becky) —Let Me Love You (A)
(Darling Jill) —Artist Model
(Darling Jill) (B) —First Date
(Date Night) —China Doll
Dating Game, The —M, BF, 1966
David Boy —3M, 1968
Day at the Office, A —M, F, 1967
(Deal, The) —Burglar Makes A Deal, The
(Debbie) (B) —Rod Rammer
(Debbie's Doctor) —Nympho, The
(Dee) (A) —Fly, The
Delivery, The —2M, F, 1956-62
Delivery Boy (A) —M, BM, F, 1963-65
Delivery Boy (B) —M, F, 1966
(Delivery Boy) (C) —Cheater, The
(Delivery Kid) —Grocer Boy, The
(Dentist, The) (A) —Slow Fire Dentist
Dentist, The (B) —M, F, 1947-48
Desert, The —M, 2F, 1949-53
Desires —M, 2F, Germany, 1952-53
Desk, The (A) —M, F, 1959-62
(Desk) (B) —The Bends
(Detective, The) —Detective One Hung Low
Detective One Hung Low —2M, F, 1948-52
(Deuces Wild) —Two Girls Alone
Dice Diddlers —BM, M, BF, F, 1966

Dice Game (A) —2M, 2F, 1950-55
(Dice Game) (B) —Coming Out
Dildo Delight (B) —M, F, 1968-70
Dill Dollies —3F, England, 1966-67
Ding-A-Ling —M, F, 1960-66
Dinner for Three —2F
Dinner Time —M, 2F, 1966
(Dirty Gerty) —Drunkard's Paradise
Dirty Girls —M, 2F, England, 1966-67
Dirty Perverts (Parts I and II) —M, F, England, 1967-68
Divorce Attorney —M, F, 1966-67
Doc Black —BM, 2BF, 1932-35
(Doctor, The) (A) —Call for Dr. Handsome
(Doctor) (B) —Dr. Longpeter
Dr. Fix'em —M, F, 1958-62
(Dr. Fix It) —Dr. Fix'em
(Dr. Gunsmoke) —Call for Dr. Handsome
(Dr. Handsome) —Call for Dr. Handsome
Dr. Hardon's Injections —2M, F, 1931-36
Doctor in Bed —M, 2F, Denmark, 1970
Doctor Kildare —M, F, 1966
(Doctor Kinsey) —Kensey [sic] Report
Dr. Longpeter —M, F, 1948-55
(Dr. Love Bug) —Lady Doctor
(Dr. Penis) —Oh, Dr. Penis!
Doctor's Orders (Parts I and II) —M, F, 1951-52
Dr.'s Prescription for Love —2M, 2F, 1950-55
(Dr.'s Rx for Love) —Dr.'s Prescription for Love
Dog Fun —F, Z, England, 1968
(Dog Health) —Boxer Dog

Dog Orgy —3F, Z, England, 1966-67
(Doing a Good Job) —*Cock Sucker*
Do It at Home —2M, 1968-70
Do-It-Yourself —M, F, England, 1966
Do Me Again —M, 2F, 1968
Do Me Now —M, 2F, 1968-70
Domination of Justine —England, 1965-67
Don't Come Back (A)—M, 2F, England, 1966-67
Dornmöschen (Parts I and II)—animated cartoon, Germany or Italy, 1950s-60s
Dorothee and Anton —M, 2F, Germany, 1952-53
(Dotty Peeper) —*Threesome, The* (A)
(Dotty Twott and Zany Jane) —*Getting Warmed Up*
(Double Barrel) —*Queen High* (Part II)
Doublecross —M, F, 1964-66
Double Date —M, F, 1958-62
Double-Deck Beds —M, F, 1958-63
Double Down (A)—2M, BF, 1965-67
Double Down (B)—2M, F, 1958-62
(Double Fun) —*Vibora, La* (A)
(Do Unto Others) —*Rape in Reverse*
(Dozen Ways) —*Twelve Different Ways*
(Dream) (A)—*Fantasy*
(Dreamer, The) (A)—*Lady Dreamer*
Dreamer, The (B) (Part II)—M, F, 1958-62
(Dreamer's Interlude) —*Dancer's Interlude* (V-1)
Dream Girl (A)—M, F, Holland, 1960-66
Dream Girl, The (B)—M, F, 1966
Dream Job —M, F; 1955

Dream Lovers —M, 2F, England, 1967-68
Dreams —2M, 2F, Sweden, 1960-68
(Dream Salesman, The) —*Pricking Cherries*
Dressing Room (A)—M, F, 1965-66
(Dressing Room) (B)—*Dressing Room Scene*
Dressing Room Scene —XYM, XYF, 1966
Drunkard's Paradise —M, F, 1951-52
(Drunkard's Return) —*Drunkard's Paradise*
Drunks —M, F, 1948-52
Dumb Burglar —XM, F
Dutch Fight —M, F, Germany, 1952-53

Eager Beaver —M, F, 1958-64
(Early Duties) —*Early Riser*
Early Riser —M, F, 1951-54
Easiest Way, The —M, F, England, 1920s
Eastern Promise —M, F, England, 1966-68
(Easy Chair) —*Good Mixers* (V-1)
Easy Meet —2M, 2F, England, 1967
Easy Money —M, F, 1926-28
Eatemupski [sic]—M, F, 1955-60
Eat, Live and Be Merry —M, BF, 1965-66
(Ecstasy in Platinum) —*Paid in Full*
Egyptian Adventure, An —M, F, 1940-45
Electrician, The —M, F, 1961-62
Emergency Clinic —2M, F, 1948-52
End of Term —M, F, England, 1967-68
Engagement Party —M, F, 1958-64
English Joys —M, F, England, 1940-44
(English Picnic) —*English Joys*
English Tragedy, An —M, F, 1920-26
Entre Dos Fuegos —LM, 2LF, Cuba, 1948-55
Epic (Part I)—3M, 1963-64

133

(Epic) (Part II) —*Gary and Guy* (Part II)

Epic (Part III) —BM, M, 1963-64

Equal to Mummy —M, F, England, 1968

Erotica —3M, 3F, England, 1966-67

Errand Boy —BM, BF, F, 1964-66

Ersatz —M, 2F, Italy, 1943

Escape (V-1) —M, F, 1946-50

Escape (V-2) —M, F, 1946-50

(Escaped Prisoner) —*Prisoner Knocks at the Door!*

Escort Agency —M, F, England, 1967

Esprit de Famille (Parts I and II) —M, 2F, France, 1947-50

Eternal Triangle (Parts I and II) —M, BF, F, 1966-67

Evening At Home (A) —BM, BF, F, 1964

Evening at Home (B) —M, F, England, 1960-66

Even Thieves Do It —3M, 2F, Denmark, 1968-70

Ever Loving —M, BF, 1963-65

(Ever Ready) —*Buried Treasure*

Exchange Students —XM, XF, 1962-64

Excited —2M, 2F

Exclusive Sailor, The —2M, F, France, 1920s

Exerciser —BM, F, 1964

Exhibition —M, 2F, England, 1967-68

(Experienced Honey) —*Experienced Honeymooners*

Experienced Honeymooners —M, F, 1936-38

(Faceless Passion) —*Night at Home, A*

Fairyland —2YM, 1958-63

Faites Patienter! —M, 2F, Austria, 1927

False Pretenses —M, 2F, England, 1966-67

Family Affair, A —M, 2F, England, 1964-66

Family Fun —M, 2F, England 1967-68

Fanny —M, 2F, England, 1967-68

Fanny From Frisco —M, F, 1958-61

Fanny Hill (A) —M, 4F, 1952-56

Fanny Hill (B) —BM, BF, F, 1963-65

Fantasy —XM, F, 1950s

Farmer's Daughter —M, F, 2Z, 1930s

(Fashion Model) (Parts I and II) —*Man and Wife* (Parts I and II)

Fast Action —M, 2F, 1948-52

Father and Daughter (A) —M, F, England, 1966

Father and Daughter (B) —M, 2F, Scandinavia, 1968-70

Father Knows Best (Parts I and II) —2M, F, 1964-66

Fat Man —M, F, 1965

(Feeling Groovy) —*Crazy Time*

Fellows, The —2M

Femme au Portrait, La —M, 2F, France, 1952

Field Trip —3M, 2F, BF, 1968

Fiesta —M, 2F, 1948-52

Fifi (Parts I and II) —M, F, 1956-62

Figure Models —M, F, 1968

Filles de Loth, Les —M, 2F, France (Nathan), 1920

Fireside Lights —XM, F, 1958-62

First Audition —M, F, England, 1966-67

First Date —M, F, 1955-58

(First Fight) —*Make-Up*

Fisherman's Dream, A —M, F, 1930s

Fisherman's Luck —M, F, England, 1965-67

Fisher Woman —M, F, 1950-55

(Fishin') —Fisherman's Dream, A

Five for Sex —2M, 3F, England, 1967

Flagellation Club, The —M, F, 1950s

Flagulation [sic] —2M, BF, England, 1967-68

Flatmates —M, 2F, England, 1964-66

Flat Tire —M, F, 1940s

Fly, The —M, F, 1962-63

For After Sex —M, F, 1956-62

For Bernie —M, F, 1958-62

Forced Entry —M, 2F, Denmark, 1970

Forest Friends —M, 2F, 1968-70

Forever Limber —M, F, 1935-39

For Johnny —M, F, 1958-62

For the Love of Pete —M, F, 1962-66

(Fortunate Accident) —Accidente Afortunado, Un

'44' in Action —M, F, England, 1966-67

4-Ever Yours —2BM, 2F, 1967

Four on a Lark —2M, 2F, 1965-66

Four on a Pony —M, LM, F, LF, 1967

Four on the Floor (Parts I and II) —M, BM, 2F, 1966-67

(Foursome) —Twin Mandy

Foursome —M, 3F, Denmark, 1970

(Four Way Swap) —Four on the Floor (Part II)

(Foxey [sic] Fireman) —Foxy Fireman

Foxy Fireman —M, F, 1956-60

(Fraulein) —Clean Shave

Freak Out —4M, 5F, 1968-70

Free for All (A) —2M, 2F, 1955-58

Free for All (B) —2M, 2F, England, 1967

Free Lunch —2M, F, 1956-62

(Free Rent) —Inspiration

Free Ride, A —M, 2F, 1915

(French Dog) —Brown Bomber

French Fun —M, F,

(French Lover) (A) —Early Riser

French Lovers (B) —M, 2F

French Maid —M, F, England, 1968

French Movements —M, F, 1932-36

(French Painting) —Femme au Portrait, La

(French Playmate) —Shane (Part II)

French Style —M, F, 1962-64

French Teacher —M, 6F, France, 1920s

Fresh Meat —2M, 2F, 1966-67

(Friendly Neighbor) —Never a Dull Moment (Parts I and II)

Friendly Relations —M, F, 1965

Friend of the Young One —2F, England, 1964-66

Fruit Salad (A) (V-1) —M, 2F, 1948-52

(Fruit Salad) (A) (V-2) —Fast Action

Fruit Salad (B) —BM, F, England, 1967-68

Fuck By Notes —M, 2F, Denmark, 1970

(Fucked) —Get Fucked

Fuck Me Fuck My Friends —2M, 2F, 1968

Fuck Me I'll Never Smile Again —M, 2F, 1968

Full House —2M, 2F, 1964-66

Full Payment —M, F, 1958-62

Full Treatment —M, 2F, England, 1967

(Fun!) —Jamaica Fun!
Fun and Games —2M, 2F, England, 1968
Fun at Lunch —M, F, England, 1968
Fun City —M, XYF, 1966
Fun for 3! —M, 2F, l968-70
(Fun Land) —Jamaica Fun!
Fur Pie —2LF, Mexico, 1958-66
(Fur Piece, A) —Blimp, The
Fuzzy Wazzy [sic] the Repairman —M, F, 1968

Galant Chauffeur, Le —M, 2F, France, 1934
Games You Love to Play —M, F, 1968
Gang Bang (Part I) —M, 2F, 1966
Gary and Guy (Part I) —2BM, 1964-65
Gary and Guy (Part II) —2BM, M, 1964-65
Gay Artist, The —2M, F, 1964-66
Gay Count, The —M, F, 1932
Gay Judo —3M, 1968-70
(Gay Party) (B) —Cheater (Parts I and II)
(Gay Times) —Merry-Go-Round (Part I)
Geisha Girl —2M, F
Genie —2LM, 3LF, Mexico, l935-39
Gentleman's Paradise —M, F
George and the Blonde —M, F, 1955-56
(George and the Hillbilly) —Office Girl (Part II)
Get Fucked —2M, F, England, 1966-67
(Getting His Goat) —Goat, The
Getting There Is Half the Fun —M, BM, BF, 2F, 1967
Getting Warmed Up —2F, 1947-48
Giant Killer (A) —XBM, XF

(Giant Killer) (B) —TV Repairman (A)
Gibson Girl —M, F, 1945-49
Gigolo, The (A) —M, 2F, 1931-36
(Gigolo) (B) —Model, The
(Gigolo, The) (C) —Season's Catch
Gigs and Boys —2YF, M, Denmark, 1970
G.I. Joe Returns Home —M, F, 1951-54
(G.I. Joe the Cameraman) —Movie Camera Man
Ginny and Her Boyfriend —M, F, 1967
(Girl and Wine) —Wine Girl, The
(Girl Bang) —Gang Bang (Part I)
Girl Farm —M, 3F, 1968-70
Girlfriend, The —2M, F, England, 1967
Girl Fun —2F, 1963-66
Girl Named Beth, A —M, F, 1964-66
Girl Next Door —M, F, 1950s
Girl of My Dreams, The —M, F, 1946-48
Girl Thrill Seekers —M, 2F, 1968
Girls, Les (A) —2F, 1966-67
Girls, The (B) —3LF
Girls at Wendy's —M, 2F, 1968
Girls Next Door —3F, 1967-68
Girls of Passion —2BF, 1966
(Girls Will Be Boys) —She
Glorious Weekend —M, F, 1949-52
Goat, The —M, 3F, Z, 1920-26
(Goat Man, The) —Goat, The
(Go Go) —Dancing Party
Going Down (A) —M, F, 1930s
(G-O in Mirror) —Hot Doggie
Golden Chalice —M, F, 1968-70
Golden Shower —M, BF, F, 1937
Goldilocks and Bare —M, F, 1968

Goldilocks Rapes the Wolf (Parts I and II) —M, F, 1964-66

Golf Lesson —M, 2F, 1959-62

(Good Lay, A) —*Never a Dull Moment* (Parts I and II)

Good Mixers (V-1) —M, F, 1931-33

Good Mixers (V-2) —M, F, 1931-33

Good Time Girls —2M, 2F, England, 1965-66

Good Times —2M, 2F, 1965

Grande Bagerre, La —M, 2F, France, 1930s

(Grass Sandwich) —*Free Ride, A*

Great Love —M, 3F, 1968

(Greedy Dreams) —*Lady Dreamer*

Greek, The (A) —M, F, 1958-62

(Greek, The) (B) —*Zorba the Greek*

Greek Salad —M, F, 1968

Greek Tail —2M, 1968-70

(Greta Garbo) —*Chess*

Gretchen and Faust —2M, 2F, Germany 1920s

Grocer Boy, The (A) —M, F, 1951-55

Grocer Boy (B) (Parts I and II) —M, F, 1965-66

(Grocery Boy) (C) (Parts I and II) —*Cheater* (Parts I and II)

Groovy —2M, 2F, 1968

Gross Plans —M, F, Germany

Gruppen Sex —M, 4F, Denmark, 1970

Guessing Game —M, 2F, England, 1967

Guitar Player —M, F, 1965-67

(Gym) —*Boy Oh Boy* (Part II)

Gypsies —M, F, Mexico, 1944-55

Gypsy —2M, BF, 1962

Handy Man, The (A) —BM, BF, F, 1930s

Handy Man (B) —M, 2F, England, 1966-67

(Handyman, The) (C) —*Pee for Two*

Hangman's Night, The —M, 2F, Denmark, 1970

Happy Family —M, 2F, 1967-68

Happy Feet —M, F, 1966

(Hard to Please) —*Hot Rod in Hard to Please*

Harlem —BM, 2BF, F

(Harlem Honey) —*Tease for Two* (A)

(Harlem Hotshots) —*Three Harlem Hotshots*

Harlem Medley —2M, 2BF, 1968

Harmony in Marriage —M, F, 1967

Harry Lays Two —M, 2F, 1968-70

Hat Check Girl, The —M, F, 1965-66

Haunts of a Honey Blonde —2F, 1968-70

Have Crack Will Shack —M, F, 1964-66

(Having a Ball) —*Interlude*

(Having a Good Time) —*Interlude*

(Having Fun) —*Beach Girl* (A)

Heads Up —YM, OF, 1955-58

Heat Wave —M, OF, 1966-67

(Hellen and Jane) —*Year 1965*

Hell Fire Club —2M, F, Denmark, 1970

Hell's Angel —M, F, 1966

Help, Mouse! —M, F, 1958-63

Help Wanted (Part I) —2F, 1965-66

Help Wanted (Part II) —M, 2F, 1965-66

Her Daughter Raped —2XM, 2F, England, 1964-66

(Here Comes the Clown) —*Burlesque Queen*

Her Maid Raped —2M, BF, F, England, 1966-67

Her Victim —2F, England, 1966-67

Highway Romance, A —M, F, 1930s
Hillbillies' Frolics —M, F, 1930s
(Hip Hitch Hiker) —Modern Hitch Hiker, A
Hippies Flower Party (Part I) —3M, 2F, 1967-68
Hippies Flower Party (Part II) —3M, 3F, 1967-68
Hippy Sex —M, 2F, Denmark, 1970
Hired Hand —M, F, 1966-67
(Hitch Hiker) (A) —Highway Romance, A
Hitch Hiker (D) —M, F, England, 1965-67
(Hole in One) —Clean Shave
Holiday Inn —M, F, 1966
Hollywood Honeymoon —M, 2F, 1950-55
(Hollywood Model) —Night to Remember (V-I)
(Home at Last) —Doctor's Orders
Home Coming —M, F, 1950s
Home Cookin' —M, F, 1966-67
Home from School —2M, F, England, 1963-66
Home Movies —M, F, 1950-55
Home on Leave (Parts I and II) —M, F, 1965-66
(Homework) (B) —Exchange Students
Homework (C) —M, 2F, England, 1966-67
(Homework Helper) —Private Tutor
Honeymoon, The —M, F, 1968
Honeymoon Cottage —M, F, 1948-50
Honeymooners (A) —M, F, 1958-62
(Honeymooners) (B) —Trial Marriage
Honeymoon Hell —M, F, 1968
(Hong Cong [sic] Caper) —Oriental's Dream, An

Hooker's Hooka —M, 2F, 1968
(Horse Doctor) —Dr. Longpeter
(Hot) —100% Lust
Hot Chicks —2F, 1947-48
Hot Dog (A) —3F, 1920-23
Hot Doggie —XM, 2M, 3F, 1960-64
Hotel —M, 2F, England, 1966-67
(Hotel Detective) —Detective One Hung Low
(Hot Hotel) —Detective One Hung Low
Hot Line —2M, F, England, 1968
(Hot Night) —One Hot Night
Hot Panties —M, F, 1966-67
Hot Party —2M, 2F, 1928-33
Hot Pussy —M, 2F, 1930s
Hot Rod —M, F, Cuba, 1949-56
Hot Rod in Hard to Please —M, 5F, 1948-53
(Hot Stuff) (A) —Pleasure Bent
Hot Stuff (B) —M, LF, 1958-62
(Hot Stuff) (C) —Temptress
(Hot Stuff) (D) (V-I) —Twatters in "Hot stuff" (V-1)
(Hot Stuff) (D) (V-2) —Twatters in "Hot Stuff" (V-2)
(Hot Thing) (Parts I and II) —Hot Tung (Parts I and II)
Hot Tung [sic] (Parts I and II) —M, F, 1968-70
(House Call) —Nympho, The
House Painter (Parts I and II) —M, F, 1967
Housewife at Play —F, BF, 1964-66
How Deep Is My Valley —BM, F, 1965-66
How Sweet It Is —M, F, 1963-65
(How to Become a Movie Star) —Casting Couch

(How to Fuck) —Sex Teacher, The
(How to Hold a Husband) (A) —Artist, The
(How to Hold a Husband) (B) —Night to Remember, A (V-2)
"H.P." Man, The —2M, F, England, 1966-67
Humiliation —M, 2F, England, 1966-67
(Hungry Newlyweds, The) —Newlyweds, The (B) (Parts I and II)
Hunter and His Dog, A —2LM, 2LF, Z, Mexico, 1935-39
Hycock's Dancing School —M, 2F, 1932-36
Hypnotist, The —M, BF, F, 1932-36

Iceman, The —M, F, 1920-30
Idiot, The —XM, F, 1948-49
I'll Cry Tomorrow —M, F, 1950-55
I'm a Comin' —M, F, Z, 1968
I Married Joan —M, F, 1958-62
(Immediate Payment) —Delivery Boy (A)
(I'm So Hot) —Modelo para la Pintora, Un
Incest (A) —M, F, England, 1964-66
Incest (B) —M, 2F, England, 1968
Incestral [sic] Home —2M, 2F, England, 1968-70
Indian Giver —2M, F, England, 1958-62
Indifferent —M, F, 1948-52
In Drag —XM, M, England, 1967
Inez —BM, BF
Inspiration —M, F, 1940s
Instructor, The —M, 2BF, 1948-52
Insurance Salesman —M, F, 1967
Interlude —2M, F, 1945-49
Intermezzo —2M, F, 1965-66

In the Name of Odin —group, Denmark, 1970
(In Time) —Private Tutor
Intoxication (Parts I and II) —M, 3F, England, 1967-68
Intruder, The —2M, F, 1930s
Inutile Stratagème —M, 2F, France, 1924
Invitation —M, F, England, 1968
Irene Gets an Idea —M, 2F, 1967
Ironing Board, The —M, F, 1958-63
(Island Queen) —Anniversary Party
It's All for Fun —M, 2F, 1968
I Want More —M, F, 1968-70
I Want Two —2M, F, England, 1967-68

Jack the Sniffer —M, F, 1964-66
Jamaica Fun! —M, BM, F, BF, 1967
Jam Session —M, F
(Jane's Love Life) —Love Affairs of Jane Winslow, The
Jane's Masseur —2F, 1950-60
(Jane Winslow) —Love Affairs of Jane Winslow, The
(Japanese Magician) —Oriental's Dream, An
Jap Whip —OM, OF, Japan, 1960s
Jassmore College —M, F
Jazz Mania —M, F, 1932-36
(Jealous Roommate) —Twin Mandy
Jealous Sisters —2M, 2F, England, 1964-66
Jeff's Folly —2M, 2F, 1968
Jerry and Glen —M, F, 1956
Jeux d'Amour, Les —3M, France, 1968-70
Je Verbalise —2M, F, France (Nathan), 1923
(Jig Saw) —Hot Doggie

(Jig Time) —Two Nights and a Day (V-1)
Jitterbug —M, F, 1966
Job Training —M, F, 1965-67
(Johnny Ringo) —The Barker
Johnny Twatsucker —M, F, 1965-66
(Joining the Party) —Gang Bang (Part I)
(Josephine) —Man and Wife
Judo Lesson —2M, 2F, Denmark, 1970
Junkies and the Nightmare, The —3M, F, 1948-52
Just Fooling Around —M, F, 1951-53
(Justine) —Domination of Justine
Just Wee Boys (Parts I and II) —3M, 1966-68
Just Wee Girls —3LF, 1950

Keep It Kinky —2YM, 2YF, England, 1968
Kensey [sic] Report —M, F, 1952-54
(Kerry Hop) —Young Couple (A)
(Kidnapped) —Love Affairs of Jane Winslow, The
Kid Sister —M, F, 1946-52
Killer-Diller —M, F, 1960-65
Kill the Giant —M, F, 1960-65
King-Hyme Stud —M, 2F, 1968
King Size —2F,
Kinky Couples —2M, 2F, England, 1966-67
Kinky Fun —2M, 2F, England, 1968
Kinky Les —3F, England, 1966-67
Kinky Lovers —M, F, England, 1966-67
Kinky Sisters —M, 2F, England, 1968
(Kinsey Report) (A) —Kensey [sic] Report
Kinsey Report, The (B) —M, F, 1965-66
(Kismet) —Kinky Couples

(Kiss) —Kiss My Cunt
Kiss My Cunt —2M, 2F, 1965-66
Kitchen Games —BM, BF, 1964-66
Kittens, The —M, 2F, 1966-68
KKK Nightriders —XM, BF, 1939
Knight of Love —AM, F, 1956-62
Knockout —BM, F, 1964
(Krazy Kat House) —Crazy Cat House
Kutchur Balzoff [sic] —3LF, 1950s
Kutie Kut Ups [sic] —3LF, 1950s

(Lady and the Maid, The) —Señora y la Criada, La
Lady Barber —M, BF, 1963-66
Lady Burglar —M, XF, 1965
Lady Doctor —M, F, 1951-54
Lady Dreamer —2M, F, 1951-54
Lady in Blue —M, F, 1967
(Lady in Blue) (Part II) —Platinum Blonde
Lady Lovers —2F, England, 1968
Lady M —3M, F, Denmark, 1969-70
Lady's Choice —M, F, 1960s
Lapping —M, F, 1960-64
Lapping Dog —F, Z, 1960-64
Lappin' It Up —2M, 2F, 1960-64
Last Exit —M, F, England, 1966-68
Late Date —M, F, 1949-52
(Late for Work) (A) —Love Nest, The (A)
Late for Work (B) —2M, F, 1959-62
Latex Salesman —M, F, 1958
Latin Lupe Lou (V-1) —LM, LF, 1966
Latin Lupe Lou (V-2) —LM, LF, 1966
Laura Really Digs It —LM, M, LF, F, 1967

Lazy Saturday, A —2M, 2F

Leaky Sink —M, BM, F, 1966

(Lean Look) —Clean Floors

Lecherous Tailor, The —M, 2F, Denmark, 1970

Leçon d'Amour —M, 2F, France (Nathan), 1922

(Legs First) —Legs Up for Sex

Legs Up for Sex —M, F, England, 1967-68

Les . . . —2F, 1967

Lesbian Candle —2F, 1968

(Lesbian Club) —Busy Lesbian Club

Lesbian Desires —2F, England, 1966-67

Lesbian Paradise, A —M, 2F, 1939-41

(Lesbians, The) —Caught By Surprise (Parts I and II)

Lesbian Sister —2F, England, 1968

Lesbian Trio —3F, England, 1965-66

Les Delight —M, 2F, England, 1967

(Lessons in Jazz) —Blends

Let Me Have a Piece Baby —M, 2F, 1968

Let Me Love You (A) —XM, 2F

(Let Me Love You) (B) —Mary Ann

Let Me Show You —BM, F, 1967

Let's Get Started —M, F, 1962-63

Letter from Maisie —M, F, 1940-45

Let Us and Tomatoes —M, 2F, 1968

Levantador, El —LM, 2LF, Cuba, 1950-55

(Life) —Lovers (B)

Life on the Road—2M, F, 1935-45

(Light Bulb) —Busy Girl

(Lil's Place) —Quiet Night at Lil's Place, A

Limbo —BM, 3BF, Denmark, 1969-70

Linda Loves Her —F, LF, 1967

Lip Service —M, BF, 1963-65

Little Bird Told Me, A —2F, 1940-50

Little Eva —M, F, 1920-30

Little Girl Lost —2M, F, England, 1966

(Little Sister) —Esprit de Famille

Live Show —M, 2F, England, 1968

Living for Kicks —2M, F, England, 1965-67

(Liz) —Candy

Load of Fun —XM, F, 1958-64

Locksmith, The —M, F, BF, 1966

Loin du Bal —M, 2F, Austria, 1928

London Bridge —M, F, 1930s

(London Lovers) —Coloured Rainbow

(London Party) —Surprise (A)

Lonely —M, F, 1966

(Lonely Girl) —Odd Man In (Part I)

Lonesum [sic] Janet—M, F, 1965

Long and White —XM, F, 1960-63

Long John and Tight Mary —M, F, 1947-48

Losing Game, The —M, F, 1955-56

Loveable Cheat (Parts I and II) —M, F, 1958-62

Love Affairs of Jane Winslow, The —2M, 2F, 1935-40

(Love Bug) (A)—Lady Doctor

(Love Bug) (B)—Unexpected Company (A) (Parts I and II)

(Love Burglar) —Burglar Boy

Love By Appointment—M, BF, 1965-6

Love Expert —M, BF, England, 1964-66

Love Flat —M, F, Germany, 1960-62

(Love for Breakfast) —Greek Salad

(Love for Money) —Love for Sale (B)

141

Love for Sale (A) (Parts I and II) —BM, F, 1964-66

Love for Sale (B) —M, 2F, England, 1967-68

Love Game —

Love Hungry —M, F, 1950s

(Love in Mexico) —*Romance Campesino, Un*

Love in the Afternoon —M, F, 1968

Love Nest, The (A) —M, F, 1946-52

Love Nest, The (B) (Parts I and II) —M, 3F, 1965-66

(Love on the Rocks) —*A Highway Romance*

Lover, The (A) —XM, XF, 1962-64

Lovers (B) —2M, F, 1958-62

(Lovers) (E) —*Trial Marriage*

Lovers, The (C) —2M, F, 1958-64

Lovers, The (D) —M, F, 1966-67

Lover's Delight —M, F, 1950s

Love Scene, A (Part I) —M, 2F, 1966

Love Scene, A (Part II) —2F, 1966

Love Slave (Parts I, II, and III) —BF, F, 1966

L.S.M.F.T. —2F, 1964-66

Lucile [sic] *Ball* —M, F, 1967

Luckey —M, F, 1967-68

Lucky Boys —M, BM, F, England, 1968

Lucky Break —M, 2F, England, 1964-66

Lucky Girl —2M, F, England, 1968

(Lucky Pete) —*Big Event,, The*

(Lucky Pilot) —*Aviator, The*

(Lucky Porter) —*Swinging Hotel*

Lucky Prowler —M, 2F, 1966-69

Lusious [sic] *Lesbians* —2F, England, 1967

Lust Lady —M, 2F, 1950s

(Mable's Room) —*Hot Rod in Hard to Please*

Madame Butterfly —2M, 2F, France (Nathan), 1920

Magazine Collector —M, F, 1931

Magazine Sales Girl —M, BF, 1966

Magic —M, BF, F, 1966

Magician, The —M, F, 1930s

Magic Room —M, F, 1964-66

Maid, The —M, BF, 1964-66

(Maiden's Wish, A) —*Hot Stuff* (B)

Maid Is Made, The —M, 2F, 1964-66

Maid's Delight —2F, England, 1966-67

Maid to Measure —M, 2F, England, 1968

Maisie —M, F, 1940-45

Maitresse du Capitaine de Meydeux, La —2M, F, France, 1924

(Make Love) —*English Joys*

(Make Up) —*Rin-Tin-Tin Mexicano*

Making Poppy Love —M, F, 1958-62

Making the Maid —M, BF, England, 1965-66

Male Prostitute, The —M, F, 1965-66

(Mamie, George and Rex) —*Rascal Rex*

Man and Man —7M, 1963-66

Man and Wife (Parts I and II) —M, F, 1965-66

Man Called Sex, A —BM, F, 1966-67

Man Crazy —2M, F, England, 1967

(Man Game) —*Odd Man In* (Part II)

Man Hungry —2M, F, England, 1964-66

Maniac, The —XM, F, 1965-66

Manoir des Chatiments, Le —M, 2F, France, 1948

Man Power —M, F, 1960-67

Man Raped —M, F, 1969-72

(Man's Best Friend) —*Boxer Dog*

Man Shortage —2XF, 1939-41

(Man Wanted) —*Help Wanted*

(Margie) (A) —*One Hot Night*

(Margie in 'One Hot Night') —*One Hot Night*

Marks [sic] Bros. —2M, 2F, 1963-65

Mary Ann—M, F, 1950-55

(Mary Poppin) —Who is Mary Poppin'?

(Masked Marvel) —Nympho, The

Masked Muff Divers, The —2XF

Masked Rape (A) —XM, F, 1930s

Masked Rape (B) —M, 2F, 1948-52

Masquerading Balls —2M, F, 1947-50

(Massage) —Massage Treatment

Massages —M, 2F, France, 1937

Massage Treatment —M, 2F, England, 1962-66

(Matinee) —My Wife's Best Friend (Part II)

Matinee Idol —M, 2F, 1930s

(Mattress Joy) —Drunkard's Paradise

(Maxie and His Friends) —Indian Giver

Maxine and Billy —2F, 1964-66

(Mazaje) —Jane's Masseur

(Meat Loaf) —Bathroom Frolics

Mecktoub —3M, 2F, France (Nathan), 1920

Meditation —M, F, 1968

(Memoirs of a Hollywood Blonde) —Night at Home, A

Men —2M, England, 1964-67

Ménage à Trois —M, F, 1967-69

Men Are Everything —M, F, 1964-66

Merry-Go-Round (Parts I and II) —2XM, F, 1947-51

(Merry Hop) —Young Couple (A)

Messe Noire —M, 10F, France, 1928

(Meter Reader) —Peter the Meter Reader

Mexican Big Dick —BM, BF

(Mexican Dance) —Mexican Dream

Mexican Dog —2F, Z, Mexico, 1930s

Mexican Dream —3M, F, 2Z, Mexico 1935-39

Mexican Honeymoon —2M, F, Mexico, 1935-39

(Mexican Lady and Dog) —Rin-Tin-Tin Mexicano

(Mexican Lover) —Como Quiere un Mexicano

Mexican Mix-Up —3F, Mexico, 1945

(Mexican Romance) —Romance Campesino, Un

(Mexican Thrills) —Romance Campesino, Un

(Mexican Wedding) —Mexican Honeymoon

(Mexican Wood Chopper) —Romance Campesino, Un

(Mexican Woodsman) —Romance Campesino, Un

(Mice Will Play) —While the Cat's Away

Michelangelo —M, F, 1965-66

Mickey and Dickie —2M, F, 1935-45

Mickey Fin [sic] —M, F, 1967-69

(Midnight Romp) —Pam (A)

(Midnight Snack) —Newlyweds, The (B) (Part II)

Midnight Til Dawn —M, 2F, 1947-48

Mirror on the Wall, The —M, F, 1959-62

Miss-Conduct —2F, England, 1968

(Miss Hot-Shot) —Make-Up

Miss Hypnotist —M, F, 1959-62

Miss Lonely —2M, F, 1965-66

(Miss Love Bug) —Lady Doctor

(Miss Park Avenue) —Golden Shower

Mr. Fixit (A) —M, BF, 1964-66

(Mr. Fixit) (B) —Electrician, The

Mr. Pilgrim's Progress —M, 2F, England, 1966-67

Mixed Feelings —M, 2F, England, 1968

Mixed Relations —3M, 2F, 1921

Mix Up —M, BF, F, 1966

Model, The—M, F, 1960-66

(Model and the Painter, The) —Modelo para la
   Pintora, Un

(Model Girl) —Camera Bug

Modelo para la Pintora, Un—LM, LF, Cuba,
   1950-56

Model T Days —M, F, 1930s

Modern Art of Love —M, 3F, 1930s

Modern Gigolo —M, 2F, 1928

Modern Hitchhiker, A—M, F, 1936-39

Modern Hotel —2M, F, 1948

Modern Magician, The —M, F, 1930s

(Modern Motel) —Motel Moderne (V-2)

Modern Pirates —M, 5F, 1930s

Modern Romance —M, F, 1950-55

Modistes, Les —M, 3F, France (Dominique),
   1923

Moine, Le —2M, F, France (Nathan), 1922

Monkey Business —2M, F, France 1930s

Monsieur a Sonné —M, F, France, 1942

Moods of Nature(Part I) —2F, 1948-50

Moods of Nature (Part II) —3F, 1948-50

More Arts and Crafts —M, 2F, England,
   1966-67

(More Beatnick Bedlam) —Beatnick Bedlam
   (Part II)

More Fun and Games —2M, 3F, England,
   1964-66

More Suds and Sex—M, F, England, 1968

Morning After, The —M, F, 1950s

(Mortimer Snerd) —Christmas Dream

Mortimer the Salesman —XM, F, 1939-43

Motel Moderne (V-1) —M, F, 1951-54

Motel Moderne (V-2) —M, F, 1951-54

Mother and Daughter —M, BM, 2F, England,
   1966-67

(Mother Fucker, The) —Caught in the Act

Mousetrap Repairman —M, F, BF, 1930s

Movie Camera Man —M, F, 1937-41

(Movie Director) —Casting Couch

Movie Star Liz —M, 2F

Mujer Invertida, Una —M, 3F, Mexico

Mundo al Reves, El —2M, Mexico, 1942

Music Master (Parts I and II) —2M, F, England, 1965-67

Musique de Chambre —2M, F, France
   (Nathan), 1922

(My Angry Sister) —My Sister Eileen (Part II)

My Best Friend —2M, F, 1968-70

(My Buddy and Me) —Zorba the Greek

My Friend —2M, F, 1968-70

My Hero —M, F, 1965

My Love Affair with the Milkman —M, F, 1967

My Passionate Wife —M, BF, 1966

My Sister Eileen (Parts I and II) —M, F,
   1965-66

Mystères du Couvent, Les —3M, 5F, France,
   1928

My Ticklish Girlfriend—M, F, 1967

My Wife —M, F, 1967

My Wife's Best Friend (Parts I and II) —M, F,
   1965-66

My Young Sister —M, 2F, England, 1966

(Nancy) —Love Hungry

Natives, The —2LF, Mexico, 1965-68

Natural, A —2M, 2F, 1956-61

Natural Break, A —M, F, England, 1965-66

Nature Boy —BM, BF, 1949

Naughty French —3M, 4F, 1955-65

Naughty Girl —M, F, England, 1967

(Naughty Kitty) —*Ruthie* (A)

Navy Larks —2M, 2F, England, 1967

Negro and the Maid, The —BM, 2F, Denmark, 1969-70

(Negro Dancer) —*Dancer's Interlude* (V-1)

Nelson's Column —2M, BF, England, 1964-66

Never a Dull Moment (Parts I and II) —M, F, 1955-58

(New Cartoon) —*Buried Treasure*

New Civil Rights Act —BM, F, 1966

New Frolic, A —M, F, 1965-66

Newlyweds (A) —M, F, 1952-56

Newlyweds (B) (Parts I and II) —M, F, 1965-66

(New Strip Poker) —*Strip Poker* (A)

(New Ways) —*Merry-Go-Round* (Part II)

New York Honeymoon —M, F, 1946-50

(N.Y. Maid by Hellen and Jane) —*Year 1965*

(Nice and Big) —*Chance Inesperado, Un*

Nice and Easy —2M, F, 1961-67

(Nigger Lovers) —*Errand Boy*

Night at Home, A —M, F, 1930s

Night Club —M, 2F, 1930-37

Night in a Turkish Harem —3M, 2F, 1920-29

Night in Harlem —M, 2F, BF

Nightmare (B) —XM, M, F, 1965

Night School (Parts I and II) —2M, F, 1948-52

Night Spot —2M, F, England, 1968

Night to Remember (V-1) —2M, 2F, 1955-58

Night to Remember (V-2) —2M, 2F, 1955-58

Night to Remember (V-3) —M, F, 1955-58

Night with a Sailor, A —M, F, 1950-54

(Nina) —*The Big Event* (A)

(No Hooks) —*Good Mixers* (V-2)

Noir Vaut Deux Blanches, Un —BM, 2F, France, 1935

No Mercy for Susan —3F, England, 1968

Notaciario de Actualidades —M, F, Mexico, 1950

Nouvelle Bonne A Tout Faire, La —M, F, France (Dominique), 1924

Nouvelle Secrétaire, La —M, 2F, 1937

Novios Impacientes —M, F, Cuba, 1950-52

Nudie Movies! —AM, YM, 2YF, 1962-63

Nudist Bar —M, F, France, 1931

Nuits de Prince —M, F, France, 1954

(Nun's Habit, The) —*Nun's Story, The*

Nun's Story, The (Parts I and II) —M, F, 1949-52

(Nupitals of Cecilia, The) —*Sponsali di Cicilla, Gli*

Nurse Penny and Co. (Parts I and II) —XM, 2F, England, 1966-67

('Nuts' to You —*Motel Moderne* (V-1)

Nylon Man, The (Parts I and II) —M, F, 1940s

(Nymph and Her Anxious Mum) —*Changing Partners*

Nymphettes —2M, 2F, England, 1966-67

Nympho, The —XM, F, 1961-62

Nympho Nurses—M, 3F, England, 1966-67

Odd Man In (Parts I and II)—2M, F, 1965-66

(Of Course, Spunky)—*Dancing Teacher* (B)

Office Girl (Parts I and II)—M, F, 1955-56

(Office Girl's Dream)—*Pricking Cherries*

(Office Girl's Night at Home)—*Night to Remember, A* (V-3)

Office Wife—M, F, Mexico, 1940s

Office Worker—M, F

Oh, Doctor!—M, F, 1930s

Oh, Dr. Penis—M, 2F, 1948-52

Old Fashioned (Parts I and II)—M, F,

(Old Story)—*Inspiration*

(Old Swimmin' Hole)—*Fisherman's Dream, A*

O' My Pussy—2YF, Denmark, 1970

One Dark Knight—BM, AF, 1955-59

One Enchanted Evening—M, F, 1948-58

(One Evening)—*One Enchanted Evening*

One Eyed Queens Are Fucked—2M, F, 1968

One for Two—M, 2F, England, 1966

One Hot Night—M, F, 1940s

100% Lust—2M, F, England, 1965-66

One Sunday Morn—XM, 3XF, Z, 1930s

Onesy, Twosy, Threese—2M, 2F, 1968

(On Leave)—*Night with a Sailor, A*

On Livre en Ville—M, F, France (Dominique), 1930

Only Billy Missing—BF, F, 1967-68

(Only Thing, The)—*Daily Duty*

(On the Couch)—*Natural Break, A*

0069, The Man from Uncle—M, BF, 1965-66

(Ophelia's Way)—*Pricking Cherries*

(Opium Den)—*Junkies and the Nightmare, The*

Orgies Coloniales—2M, F, Spain, 1915-20

Orgy (A)—2M, 2F, England, 1967

Orgy (B)—2M, 3F, 1968-70

(Orgy and Bess)—*Sammy's Choice*

Oriental's Dream, An—M, OM, OF, Japan, 1950-55

Other Young Ones, The—M, F, England, 1964-66

(Our Daughter)—*Our Teenage Daughter*

Our Gang—5LM, 1955-65

(Our Honeymoon Pictures)—*Night to Remember* (V-2)

Our Little Angel—M, F, 1967

Our Teenage Daughter—M, 2F, 1940-45

(Our Wedding Pictures)—*Night to Remember* (V-2)

Out of Sight—2M, F, 1968

Out of Town—M, F, England, 1966-67

Over Here, Rover—2F, Z, 1962-66

(Ozark Ike)—*Forever Limber*

Paid in Full—2M, F, 1930-36

(Pair of Queens)—*Queen High* (Part II)

Pajama Game—M, 2F, 1965

Pam (A)—M, F, 1959-62

Pam (B)—M, F, 1955-65

(Pancho) —Como Quiere un Mexicano
Panties for Sale —M, F, 1940-50
Pants Set, The —2M, F, 1959-62
(Papa Away Mama Play) (B) —Paid in Full
Paris After Dark —2M, F, 1945-50
(Parlor Date) —Saturday Night in Harlem
Part-Time Job —M, F, England, 1964-66
(Party) (A) —Dancing Party
Party, The (B) (Parts I and II) —2M, 3F, 1968
(Party Fun) —Pussy Galore (B)
Party Kicks —M, 2F, England, 1967
(Party Kinks) —Party Kicks
Party of Four —2M, 2F, 1960-65
(Party Partners) —Changing Partners
Party Time —M, F, 1965
Passionate Patient —M, F, 1964-66
Passionate Virgin (Parts I and II) —M, F, 1966-67
Patient —M, F, England, 1964-66
Pause that Refreshes, The —M, F, 1960-65
Paying the Bills —M, F, 1958-63
Payment in Full —2BM, F, 1968-70
Payoff, The —M, F, 1940s
Pecker Head Frolics —M, 2F, 1930s
Pee for Two —M, F, 1930s
(Peeper, The) —Window Peeper
Peeping Jane —M, 2F, England, 1968
Peeping Tom —M, F, Germany, 1960s
Peg's Party —2M, F, 1958-63
Peintre, Le —M, 2F, France (Dominique), 1923
Pendant l'Entr'acte —M, 2F, France (Dominique), 1923

Penny's Birthday Party (Parts I and II) —3M, 3F, England, 1966-67
People Eaters, The —AM, XYF
(Perro Masajista, El) —Mexican Dog, The
Personal Touch —M, F, England, 1966-68
Perversion —2M, F, England, 1966-67
Perverted Dentist, The —M, BF, F, Denmark, 1970
Perverts —2M, F, England, 1964-67
(Pete on the Spot) —Adventures of Pete the Tramp, The
Peter Loves Mary —M, F, 1958-62
Peter Spirit, The —M, F, 1966
(Peter the Meater Eater) —Peter the Meter Reader
Peter the Meter Reader —M, F, 1947-55
(Pete's Apartment) —Picolo [sic] Pete
(Pete the Tramp) —Adventures of Pete the Tramp, The
Petit Conte de Noël —M, 3F, France, 1950
Petite Fleur —2M, OF, F, Denmark, 1970
Phallus '68 —M, F, England, 1968
Phantom Fucker —M, XM, 3F, England, 1966
(Phone Call) —Cover Girl
(Photographer, The) (A) —Paris After Dark
(Photographer) (C) —Ding-A-Ling
(Photographer's Delight) —Camera Bug
Photo Session —2M, F, England, 1964-66
Piano Teacher, The —M, F, Holland, 1964-66
Pick Up (A) —M, F, 1923
Pick Up (B) —M, F, 1950-55
Pick Ups (C) —2M, 2F, 1958-63

147

(*Picnic*) (*A*) —*A Modern Hitch Hicker*

(*Picnic*) (*B*) —*Unexpected Company* (*A*) (Parts I and II)

Picolo [sic] *Pete* —2M, F, 1930s

Piece Corp. —BM, F, 1965-66

(*Pig Tails*) —*Strange Love*

Pink Pussycat —M, F, 1958-61

Plaisirs Champetres —M, 2F, France, 1936

Plating is an Art —M, F, England, 1968

Platinum Blonde —M, F, 1967-69

Playboy —M, 2F, 1966

Playboys —2M, BF, England, 1968

Playful —M, F, 1966

(*Playgirl*) —*While the Cat's Away*

(*Playing House*) (*A*) —*Sleep Walker* (*A*) (Part II)

Playing House (*B*) —2M, F, 1962-63

Playmate —M, F, 1964-66

Playmates —M, 2F, 1956-58

Pleasure Bent —M, F, 1948-52

(*Pleasure Island*) —*Trip to Pleasure Island* (Parts I and II)

Plein Air —M, F, France/Germany, 1937

(*Plumber, The*) (*A*) —*Plumber Does a Little Plumbing, The*

(*Plumber, The*) (*B*) —*Darkie Rhythm*

Plumber Does a Little Plumbing, The —M, F, 1930s

Plumber's Helper, The —M, F, 1962-63

Plumber's Son —M, F, 1950s

(*Poker*) —*Strip Poker* (*C*)

(*Poker Game*) —*Strip Poker* (*D*)

Poker Original, Un —3M, 2F, France, 1947

Policiaca —M, F, Mexico, 1950

Pony Tail —2M, F, 1962-63

(*Portrait of a Woman*) —*Femme au Portrait, La*

Potent Painter, The —M, F, Denmark, 1970

(*Potty Peeper*) —*Chance Inesperado, Un*

Preparation, The —2M, F, 1959-62

(*Presenting Darling Becky*) —*Let Me Love You* (*A*)

Presenting Tabu —F, BF

(*Pretty Pup*) —*Super Dog*

Preview —2M, F, 1958-62

Pricking Cherries —M, F, 1930-37

Prick Teaser (Parts I and II) —M, F, 1965-66

(*Priest, The*) —*Mujer Invertida, Una*

Prince et le Groom, Le —M, 2F, France (Dominique), 1924

Prisoner Knocks at the Door! —2M, Sweden, 1960-70

(*Private Lives of the Sexy Sexteens*) —*Sexy Sexteens,* (Part II)

(*Private Tuition*) —*Private Tutor*

Private Tutor —M, F, England, 1960-64

Pro, The —2M, F, 1958-62

Professional Aptitute Test by Intra-Vaginal Sounding —2M, 2F, England, 1945

Professionals, The —OF, BF, 1967

Professor, The —M, 2F, 1967

(*Prop Boy and the Starlet, The*) —*Strictly Union*

(*Proud Flesh*) —*Long and White*

Proud Girl —M, F, 1958-62

Prowler, The —XM, XF, 1965-67

Psychiatrist, The —2M, F, XBF, 1964-66

Psycho Sex —2M, F, 1968-70

Pumping Pup, The —M, F, Z, 1966

Punishment (A) —M, F, England, 1964-66
Punishment (B) —M, 2F, England, 1966
Punishment for Naughty Girls —4F, England, 1968
(Punks) —Three Honeys
(Pushing Sales) —Tease for Two (A)
Pussy Club —M, 2F, England, 1966-67
Pussy Galore (A) —M, F, 1966
Pussy Galore (B) —M, 2F, England, 1966-67

Quartet (A) —4M, Sweden, 1963-67
Quartet (B) —2M, 2F, 1968-70
Queen for a Day —M, F, 1958-62
Queen High (Parts I and II) —2M, 2F, 1965-66
(Queer) —She Man
Quiet Night at Lil's Place, A —2M, F, BF, 1965-66

Rack, The (Parts I and II) —3M, 2F, 1958-62
Radio Man, The —M, 2F, 1931
Radio Repairman —M, F, 1945-50
(Ram Rod) —Rod Rammer
Randy —M, F, England, 1964-66
Randy Intruder —M, 2F, England, 1967-68
Rape (A) —M, F, 1956-62
Rape (B) —2LM, LF, 1966
Rape (C) —XM, F, 1962-63
Rape (D) —2M, F, England, 1966-67
Rape in Reverse —M, F, 1968
Rape in the Warehouse —M, F, 1930s
Rape is Impossible —2M, 2F, 1968
(Rape on the Floor) —Fun City
Raped by Three —3M, F, 1968

Rascal Rex —2LM, 2LF, Z, 1930s
Real Lovers —M, F, England, 1968
(Real Quickie, A) —Man and Wife (Part II)
(Real Triangle, A) —Trio, The (A)
(Reap the Harvest) —Young Blood (Part II)
Rear Admiral —England, 1960s
Rear View —England, 1960s
(Recorded Jazz) —Swimsuit Sue
(Red Dog) —Boxer Dog
Red Head Hitch Hiker —M, F, 1966
(Red Hot Masquerade) —Tiny Kuzzee
(Red Hot Red Head) —Torchy
Red Panties —M, F, 1964-66
Reducer, The —M, F, 1958-62
(Rendezvous) —Weekend Rendezvous
Rent Collector (A) —M, OF, 1966-67
Rent Collector (B) —M, 2F, England, 1966-67
Retour du Marin, Le —M, F, France, 1922
Returning Soldier —M, F, 1965-66
Reunited Foursome —2M, 2F, 1931-36
Rêve, Le —M, F, origin unknown, 1929
Reveillon —M, F, Germany, 1960-63
(Right Now) —Love Flat
Ring Up for Love —M, 2F, England, 1966-67
(Rin-Tin-Tin and His Master Grace) —One Sunday Morn
Rin-Tin-Tin Mexicano —M, F, Z, Mexico, 1930s
(Rise and Shine —Early Riser
(Road to Mandalay) —Hot Stuff (B)
(Roaring Twenties) —A Free Ride
Robber, The —2M, F, 1958-62
Robber and Susie, The —M, F, 1958-62
Rock and Roll —2LM, 2LF

Rocket—2M, F, 1963-66

Rod Rammer—M, F, 1960-65

Romance Campesino, Un—2M, F, Mexico, 1930s

Roman Orgy—2M, 5F, Denmark, 1968-70

Romp in the Woods—M, 2F, 1968

Roof Tops of New York—2F, 1929-34

Room Mates—2F, 1960s

(Room Service) (A)—Home on Leave (Part II)

Room Service (B)—M, LM, 1958-63

Room Service (C)—2M, F, England, 1968

Root Injection—M, F, 1966-67

Rose Tattoo—M, F, Holland, 1960-66

Round Robbin—2M, F, 1965

Rover Boys, The (Parts I and II)—2M, F, 1962-66

Rub Down (A)—M, F, 1958-62

Rub Down (B)—M, F, 1958-62

(Ruby Ann)—Gypsy

Rum Boogie—2BF, 1931-35

Ruthie (A)—M, F, 1948-52

Ruthie (B)—M, F, 1950s

Sacrifice, The—2M, 2F, England, 1964-67

Sadist, The—M, F, 1965-66

Sailor and Marine—2M, 1964-65

(Sailor's Days)—Exclusive Sailor, The

Saint, The—2XYM, XYF, 1966-69

Sales Lady (V-1)—M, F, 1953

Sales Lady (V-2)—M, F, 1953

Salesman and the Virgin, The—M, F, 1965-66

(Sally and Bob)—Sally and Her Boyfriend

Sally and Her Boyfriend—M, BF, 1948-52

(Sam)—Fiesta

Sammy's Choice (Parts I and II)—M, F, BF, 1966

(Sandra)—Black Market

Sandwich, The—2M, F, 1968-70

Sandy (Parts I and II—2M, F

Santa's Dream—M, 4F, 1962-66

(Santa's Ramrod)—Santa's Dream

Satan's Children—M, 3F, England, 1968

Satario, El—M, 6F, Mexico, 1934-49

Satisfied (A)—M, F, 1948-52

Satisfied (B)—BM, 2F, England, 1968

Saturday Night in Harlem—BM, BF, 1936-41

Sauna—2M, 2F, 1968-70

Scamp—M, F, 1964-66

(Scherezade and the Sultan Jr.)—Shiek, The

(Schneeflitchen Hinter den Sieben Bergen)—Snow-white the Cutie

(School Days)–Night School (Parts I and II)

School Girl (A) (Part I)—M, F, Hawaii, 1960-62

School Girl (B)—M, 2F, England, 1965-67

School Girl Buggery—M, 2F, England, 1967-68

Schoolgirl Initiation—M, YF, England, 1968

School Girl Lust—2M, 2F, England, 1966-67

School Girl Rape (Part II)—2M, 2F, England, 1964-66

Schoolgirls, The (C)—2M, 2F, England, 1966-67

School Girls Dream—2M, 3F, England, 1964-66

School Holidays—2YM, 2YF, England, 1968-70

School of Hard Cocks—M, 2BM, 3F, 1967-69

Schwänzel und Gretel—animated cartoon, Germany/Italy (?), 1950s-60s

(Scroungy Truck Driver)—Clean-Cut Truck
    Driver
(Scroungy Turned Chicken)—Clean-Cut
    Truck Driver
Season's Catch—M, 2F, 1930s
Second Hand Rose—M, F, England, 1966-68
Secret Agent—M, F, 1966-69
Secretary, The—M, F, England, 1966-67
(Secretary Gets a Raise)—Tillie the Toiler
(Secret Dreams)—Pricking Cherries
Secret Meeting—M, 2F, England, 1962-66
Secret Weapon—M, 2F, Denmark, 1970
Seducing Susan—M, F, England, 1966-67
Seduction—M, 2F, England, 1965-66
Seduction '68—M, 2F, England, 1967-68
(See You Again)—Thank You Girl
Selected Balls—3M, 2F, 1968-70
Selfish Mandy—3M, 2F, 1958-62
Señora y la Criada, La—LM, 2LF, Cuba,
    1946-56
(Señorita and Friends)—Gypsy
Sensational Movements—M, F, 1966
Services Rendered—2M, F, England, 1968
Severe Mistress—M, 2F, England, 1966
Sewing Room—M, 2F, 1968
Sex—2M, 2F, England, 1966-67
Sex American Style—M, 2BF, 2F, 1967
Sex and Lust—M, 2F, Denmark, 1970
Sex and More to Come—2M, F, 1965-66
Sex Campus—2M, F, Denmark, 1969
(Sexduction)—Seduction
Sex Flight—2M, 2F, England, 1968
Sex for Three—2M, 2F, England, 1964-66
Sex Hostess—2M, F, England, 1967
Sex-o-phone—3M, 3F, Denmark, 1969-70
Sex Orgy—2M, 2F, England, 1966-67

Sex Plantation (Parts I and II)—M, 2XBM, F,
    England, 1965-67
Sex Plot—2M, F, England, 1966
(Sex Releases Tension)—Sex and More to
    Come
Sex School—2M, 2F, England, 1964-66
Sex Teacher, The—M, F, 1967
Sex Therapist, The—M, F, England, 1965-66
Sexual Behavior of the Human Being (Parts I
    and II)—M, F, 1950s
Sexual Reflections—M, F, England, 1966-67
Sexy Clinic—M, 3F, Denmark, 1968-70
Sexy Mary Lou—M, F, 1955-60
Sexy Sexteens, The (Parts I and II)—AM,
    YM, 2YF, 1962-63
Shane (Part II)—2F, 1966
Sharing the Rent—M, 3F, Germany, 1965-67
She—2F, 1965-66
She Came This Way—M, F, 1968-70
She Man—2YLM, 1958-64
(Sherly) [sic]—Electrician, The
She's Ready—M, F,
Shiek, The [sic]—M, F, 1930s
Shirley Temple Se Enamora—M, F, Mexico,
    1935-39
Shoe Cobbler—M, F, Europe, 1930s
Should a Gentleman Offer a Lady a Joint?—M,
    2F, 1968
Shower Nymph—M, F, England, 1968
Showoff—M, F
Shrew, The—M, F, 1965-66
(Shy Ones)—Fun City
Single-O—M, F, 1960-61
Sister-in-Law—England, 1965-67
(Sister Love)—My Sister Eileen
Sister's Surprise (Parts I and II)—M, 2F, 1966

(69 Strip Set Boulevard) —*Desk, The* (A)

Sixus —3M, 3F, Denmark, 1969-70

(Sketch Artist) —*Artists and Models*

(Skipping School) —*Dancer, The*

Slave Girls —M, 2F, England, 1968

Slave of the Beast —2XM, F, England, 1965-67

Sleeping Beauty —M, F, England, 1968-70

Sleep Walker (A) (Parts I and II) —M, 2F, 1948-52

Sleep Walker (B) —2M, F, 1948-50

Sleepy (A) —3M, 2F, 1958-61

Sleepy (B) —M, BF, 1966

Slim Jim —M, F, 1962-64

Slippery Eel —M, F, Z, 1945-49

Slow Fire Dentist —M, F, 1920s

Smart Aleck (V-1) —M, 2F, 1951

Smart Aleck (V-2) (Part I) —M, F, 1951

Smooth as Velvet —M, 2F, 1955

Snack Shack —M, F, 1966-67

Snack Time —M, BF, 1966

Snake and I, The (Part I) —M, F, 1964-66

Snake and I, The (Part II) —M, 2F, 1964-66

Snow White the Cutie (Parts I and II) — animated cartoon, Germany/Italy (?), 1950s-60s

Sock it to Me —M, F, England, 1966-68

(Sock Salesman) —*Pricking Cherries*

(Soft Cock) —*Motel Moderne* (V-1)

Solo?? [sic] *Kiss My Sweet Ass* —2M, F, 1967-68

Somebody Please Help Me —M, F, 1967

(Some Like it Hot) —*Weekend Rendezvous*

Some Party —2M, 2F, 1966-67

Something Special —M, 2F, England, 1966-67

Song of the Lash —XM, XF, 1950s

Sous le Parasol —M, F, France, 1934

Souvenirs —M, F, Austria, 1928

(Spanish Delight) —*Busty*

(Spanish Hot Pants) —*Ruthie* (A)

Spanish Lust —M, 2F, England, 1968

Spanking Sadistic Love —M, F, 1966

(Specs) —*Weedhead in Muffing*

(Speed Balls) —*A Stiff Game*

Speedy Saloon —M, 2F, Denmark, 1970

(Spirit of the Family) —*Esprit de Famille*

Splish, Splash —2M, F, 1965-66

Sponsali di Cicilla, Gli —M, 2F, Italy, 1950s

(Sportie) —*Mexican Dog*

(Sports and Fun) —*A Hunter and His Dog*

(Sports Fun) —*The Desert*

(Spot) —*Lapping Dog*

Spunk Orgy —3M, F, England, 1968-70

Stag Show —M, F, 1958-62

Stage Struck —M, 2F, England, 1962-66

Stallion —BM, 3F, England, 1966-67

(Stay) —*Delivery Boy* (B)

(Stick Up) —

Stiff Game, A —M, BM, 2F, 1930s

Story of Strange Desire —2M, 2F, 1930s

(Story of Two Newlyweds) —*Honeymoon Cottage*

(Strange Desire) —*Story of Strange Desire*

Strange Hungers —M, BF, 1967

Strange Love —2F, England, 1966-67

Strange Loves —M, 2F, 1964-66

Stranger —M, XM, F, 1962-64

(Stranger, The) —*Model, The*

Strictly Union —2M, F, 1919

(Strip Dice) —*Tarzan and Boy*

Stripping for Fun—2M, F, 1965
Strip Poker (A)—M, F, 1955-56
Strip Poker (B)—2XYM, XYF, 1966
Strip Poker (C)—M, F, 1965-66
Strip Poker (D)—2M, 2F, 1955-63
(Striptease Delight)—Dancer's Interlude (V-1)
Strong Arm—2M, 1968
(Student) (A)—Love Flat
(Students) (B)—Dorothee and Anton
Stud Service—M, XF, 1966-67
Stung—M, 2F, 1968-70
Suburban Wife—2M, F, 1966
Suck A Go Go [sic]—2M, 2F, 1968
Suck A Wot! [sic]—M, 2F, 1968
Suds and Sex—M, F, England, 1966-68
(Sugar and Cream)—Pam (B)
(Sultan, The)—Shiek [sic], The
(Summer Eve)—Changing Partners
(Summer Fun)—Novios Impacientes
(Sunbather)—Glorious Weekend
Sunday Sunrise—M, F, 1964-66
Super Dog—F, Z, 1966
(Superman) (A)—Cuban Dream
Superman (B)—M, F, 1966
(Superman) (B) (Part II)—Wiggy Beats
Super Salesman—M, F, 1949-53
Super Saleswoman—2M, F, 1945-50
Supplicies, Les—M, 2F, Spain, 1936
Surprise(A)—2M, F, England, 1964-66
(Surprise) (B)—Gang Bang (Part I)
(Surprise Party)—Toot's Surprise Party
Surprise Reward—M, 2F, BF, England, 1966-67
(Susie) (A)—Sexy Mary Lou
(Susie) (B)—Robber and Susie, The

Susie Swings It (Parts I and II)—M, BF, 1966-67
(Suzy)—Gypsy
Swap—2M, 2F, 1968
Swastica [sic] in the Hole—XM, F, 1940-45
(Sweater Girl) (A)—Indian Giver
Sweater Girl (B)—M, F, 1966-67
(Swedish Massage)—French Movements
(Sweet as Honey)—Blue Plate Special (V-2)
(Sweet Dreams)—Wet Dream
Sweetheart's Revenge, The—M, F
(Swimmers)—Smart Aleck
(Swimsuit)—Mary Ann
Swimsuit Sue—M, F, 1965-66
Swingers, The—M, 2F, England, 1964-67
Swinging Debs (Part I)—2F, 1965-66
Swinging Debs (Part II)—2M, 2F, 1965-66
(Swinging Four) Swinging Debs (Part II)
Swinging Hotel (Parts I and II)—M, BM, 4F, 1966
(Swinging Party)—Village Ball (Part II)
Switchables, The (Parts I and II)—2M, 2F, 1966
Switch Hitters—M, 2F, 1967

(Take It in Trade)—Magazine Collector
Take It Off (B)—M, F, BF, 1965-66
(Take Me Back to My Boots and Sad-dles)—Variety Show
Take My Daughter!—M, 2F, England, 1966
Talk of the Town—M, F, 1934-39
(Tall Texas)—Dream Job
Tarzan and Boy—2M, 2F, 1950s
Tattoo—M, F, 1962-63
(Taxie Ride)[sic]—Lavantador, El

(Teacher) (Parts I and II)—*Night School (Parts I and II)*

Teaching the Teacher—M, F, England, 1968

Tease for Two (A)—M, BF, 1945-50

Tease for Two (B)—M, F, 1949-53

Teenage Ecstasy—2M, BF, England, 1965-66

(Teenage Lust)—*School Girl Lust*

Teenage Orgy—2M, 2F, England, 1968-70

Teenage Party—M, 2F, England, 1966-67

Teenage Rape—2M, F, England, 1968-70

Teenage Sex—2M, F, England, 1966-67

(Teen Masquerade)—*Dressing Room Scene*

(Teen Scene) (A)—*Saint, The*

Teen Scene, The (B)—M, 2F, England, 1966-67

Teens Today—2XYM, XYF, 1966

(Telegram Boy, The)—*Télégraphiste, Le*

Télégraphiste, Le—2M,2F, France, 1921-26

(Telephone Repairman)—*Jerry and Glen*

Television Repairman (B) (Parts I and II)—M, F, 1950s

Temptress—M, F, 1950s

(Tenderfoot)—*The Desert*

(Ten Different Ways)—*Art of Love, The*

Thank You Girl—M, F, England, 1966-67

Thief, The—M, F, 1966

Thief Makes Out, The—2BM, 2F, 1967

(Thieves Do It Too)—*Even Thieves Do It*

Think Different—2M, F, 1968-70

This Belongs to Davey?—M, F, 1959-62

This Gun for Hire—M, F, 1949-52

This Is the Life (A)—M, F, 1945-50

(This Is the Life) (B)—*After the Masquerade Ball*

Three Bares (B)—M, 4F, 1960-65

3 Bucks Worth—2M, 2F, 1955-65

Three Comrades—3M, 1950-60

(Three for Sex)—*Sex for Three*

Three Graces, The—3F, 1930s

Three Harlem Hotshots—BM, 2BF

Three Honeys—3M, 1962-63

Three Is a Crowd—M, 2F, 1968

Three is Not a Crowd—BM, F, BF, 1965-66

(Three of a Kind)—*Fruit Salad*

Three on a See-Saw—M, 2F, 1968-70

Three Pals—M, 2F, 1930s

Three Roses—3F, Denmark, 1968-70

3's A Crowd—2M, F, 1960-65

Three's a Crowd (C)—M, 2F, 1968

Three's Company—2M, F, England

Threesome, The (A)—M, 2F

(Threesome, The) (B)—*Surprise (A)*

Three to Get Ready—M, F, BF, 1965-66

Three V's, The—M, F, 1946-50

Three Way Lust—M, 2F, 1966

Three Way Ride, A—LM, F, LF, 1967

Three Way Split—M, 2F, 1966

(Three Women)—*Three Graces, The*

Tillie—2M, F, England, 1966-67

Tillie the Toiler—M, F, 1940s

Time for Love—M, F, 1960s

Tina and Mimi After Work—M, BM, BF, 1967

Tiny Kuzzee [sic]—XM, 2XF, 1930s

Tire Repair—M, F, 1930s

Tom and Jerry—2M, F, England, 1966-67

Tomboy (Parts I and II)—2M, F, England, 1958-63

Tonight at 8—2M, F, England, 1966-67

(Toni Twins)—Cheater (Part II)
Tony and Allan Meet—2M, 1968
Tony and Allan Together—2M, 1968
Tootsie—M, AM, F, 1956-62
Toot's Surprise Party—M, 3F, 1966
Top Banana—M, F
Topless Swimsuit—M, F, 1964
Torchy—XM, XF, 1941-46
Toreador—M, 2F, Mexico, 1935-39
Tortilla Girls—2LF, Mexico, 1948-58
Tortillas (B) (Part II)—M, 2F, Mexico, 1960-62
Torture of Tickling Tongues—3F, 1930s
To Seymour—M, F, 1958-62
Tournée des Grands-Ducs—2M, F, France (Nathan), 1923
Tree, The—M, F, 1965-66
Trial Marriage—2M, F, 1947-51
Triangle—2M, F, England, 1965-67
Triangle of Love—3M, F, 1967-68
Trio, The (A)—3M, F, 1956-62
(Trio) (B)—Lady Dreamer
Trip Around the World, A—M, F, 1932-36
Trip to Pleasure Island, A (Parts I and II)—M, F, BF, 1938
Tri-Sexual—M, 2F, England, 1966-67
Trop Curieux—M, F, Austria, 1926
Tropical Paradise—2BM, BF, Denmark, 1968-70
(Tropic Isle)—Tropic Paradise
Tropic Paradise—M, F, 1938-41
Tunnel of Love (Parts I and II)—2F, 1968-69

Turkish Delight—M, 2F, England, 1967-68
Turn on the Heat—2M, 7F, 1937
(Tuxedo Junction)—Harlem Medley
TV Casting Director—M, F, 1964-66
(TV Man)—A Natural Break
TV or Not TV—BM, F, 1964-66
TV Repairman (A)—M, F, 1962-63
Twatters in 'Hot Stuff' [sic](V-1)—M, F
Twatters in 'Hot Stuff' [sic] (V-2)—M, F
(Twat Time)—Three is Not a Crowd
Twelve Different Ways—M, F, 1948-52
(Twilight Lovers)—Black Market
Twin Beds—2LF, 1965-66
Twin Mandy—3M, 2F, 1956-62
Twin Sisters—2M, 2F, 1963-65
Twisted—BM, 2F, England, 1968
(Two Against One)—Evening At Home (A)
(Two Bachelors and the Maid)—Picolo [sic] Pete
(Two Brothers)—Mickey and Dickie
(Two Bugs and Two Bunnies) (Parts I and II)—Unexpected Company (A) (Parts I and II)
(Two Colored Girls)—Rum Boogie
(Two Colored Long Johns and White Beauty)—Two Nights and a Day (V-1)
(Two Dolls)—Two Girls Alone
Two for the Price of One—2M, F, England, 1968
Two for Tonight—2F, 1968-70
(Two French Wildcats)—Grande Bagerre, La
Two Girls Alone—2F, 1965-66
Two Heads are Better Than One—M, 2F, 1968
Two Holes in One—M, F, England

155

(Two Hot Boxes Looking for a Fireman)—
   Season's Catch
(Two Hot Chicks)—*Hot Chicks*
(Two Hungry Lovers—3M, 3F, 1952-56
Two into One—2M, F, England, 1968
Two Latins—2LF
(Two Lovers on a Sofa)—*First Date*
Two Men—2M, 1965-66
Two Nights and a Day (V-1)—2BM, F,
   1950-55
Two Nights and a Day (V-2)—2BM, F,
   1950-55
Two of a Kind—F, BF, 1960s
2 + 1—M, F, BF, 1968
2 + 2 = 69 (Parts I and II)—M, 2F, 1968
Two Reel Gay Girls [sic]—2BF, 1966-67
Two-Sided Triangle—M, 2F, 1968-70
Twosome (Part I)—M, F, 1965-66
Twosome (Part II)—M, 2F, 1965-66
Two Sweet Girls—2F, 1949-52
Two Timer, The—M, BM, F, 1945-50
(Two Times)—*Kinky Couples*
(Two Unloaded Guns)—*Paid in Full*

Undertaker's Dream, The—M, 4F, 1966
(Unexpected Caller)—*Unexpected Company*
   (B)
Unexpected Company (A) (Parts I and II)—
   2M, 2F, 1945-50
Unexpected Company (B)—M, F, 1948-52
Unexpected Guests, The—2M, 2F, England,
   1962-65
Unsatisfied Wife—M, F, 1925-35
Untouchable, The—2M, F, France, 1922-27

(Up and Down)—*Sex Plantation* (Part II)
Up the Hill—2M, BF, 1968-70
Up, Up and Away—M, 2F, England, 1968
Utility Service Deluxe—M, F, 1938-40

Valentino (V-1)—LM, LF, 1966
Valentino (V-2)—LM,LF, 1966
(Valerie's Job)—*Part-Time Job*
Variety Show—2M, 4BF, 1968-70
Varsity Girls—2M, 3F, 1948-52
Vendeur de Journaux, Le—M, F, France,
   1950-59
Vibora, La—2M, F, Cuba
Vice Probe—M, BM, 2F, 1967
Vices—group, France/Germany, 1938
Victory for the Queen—group, Denmark,
   1970
Village Ball (Parts I and II)—2M, 2F, 1966
Violence—2M, FY, FA, Denmark, 1968-70
Virgin Bride—M, F, 1948-52
Virgin's Wedding Night, The—2M, F, Den-
   mark, 1970
Vision, The—M, 3F, 1966
(Visit, A)—*One for Two*
Voleuse de Prunes, La—M, 2F, France, 1933
Voyeur, Le—M, 2F, France, 1934
Voyeurs Only—2YF, England, 1968

Waiter, The (V-1) (Parts I and II) (A)—2M,
   F, 1956-66
Waiter, The (V-2) (Parts I and II) (A)—2M,
   F, 1965-66

Waiter, The (B)—M, F, England, 1966-67
Waldes Lust—M, 2F, Germany
Wanda—M, F
(Wanda Arrives Home)—Wanda
(Wanda the Strip Artist)—Wanda
Water Sports—M, F, 1950s
Way of Life, The—2M, F, 1958-62
(Way Out)—Blackmail
Way to Valhalla, The—group, Denmark, 1970
Wedding Night (A)—M, F, 1958-62
Wedding Night (B)—2M, F, England, 1963-66
Wedding Night for Three—2M, F, Scandinavia, 1968-70
Weedhead in Muffing—M, F, 1947-51
(Weekend Fun)—Three Pals
(Week End Love)—Three Pals
Weekend Love—M, F, 1930s
Weekend Rendezvous—M, F, 1950s
(Wee Wampus)—Matinee Idol
Welcome Stranger—M, 2F, England, 1966
West Side Story (Parts I and II)—2M, F, 1964-66
Wet Dream—M, F, 1935-45
What's My Line?—M, F, 1958-62
What the Artist Missed—2M, F, 1930s
What the Butler Saw and Did—2M, F, England, 1965-67
(When the Cat's Away)—While the Cat's Away
While the Cat's Away—2M, F, 1950-55
(Whip Cream)—Stripping for Fun
Whipenpoof [sic]—M, 2F, 1968

Whipped Cream Party—M, 2F, 1967-68
(White Panties)—Change·of Plans
Who is Mary Poppin'?—M, F, 1965-66
Whoopie—M, F, 1965-66
(Why Girls Leave Home)—Smart Aleck
Wife's Lover—M, 2F, 1960-65
Wife's Revenge, A—M, F, 1945-50
Wife Swoppers [sic] (Part I)—2M, 2F, England, 1967
Wife Swoppers [sic] (Part III)—2M, 2F, England, 1967-68
Wiggy Beats—M, F, 1966
Wild Card—2M, 2F, 1968
(Wild Gal)—Rin-Tin-Tin Mexicano
Wild in the Woods—M, 2F, 1968
Wild Night (Part I)—2M, 3F, 1965-66
Wild Night (Part II)—2M, 3F, 1965
Willing and Able—M, F, BF, 1964-66
(Will Not Shrink)—My Hero
Window Peeper—BM, BF, 1960-63
Wine Girl, The—M, F, 1964-67
Witches Screw Brew!—M, 3F, 1966
Wolfman (Parts I and II)—M, 2F, 1963-66
(Woman in Black, The—Rin-Tin-Tin Mexicano
(Woman in the Portrait)—Femme au Portrait, La
(Woman Man, The)—Mujer Invertida, Una
Women—2F, Sweden, 1970
Wonders of the Unseen World—M, XF, 1927
Working on the Railroad—XBM, XBF, 1948-58
World's Fair Ways—M, F, 1962-63
(World Upside Down)—Mundo al Reves, El

Wrens at Play—M, 2F, England, 1967
Wrong Room (A)—M, F, 1964-66
Wrong Room (B)—M, F, England, 1967

Year 1965—2F, 1965
Yes I Do—2M, F, 1968-70
You and Me Darling—M, F, 1967-69
You Asked for It—2M, F, 1956-62
Young and Lusty—M, 2F, Denmark, 1968-70
Young and Super Big—M, F, 1966
Young and Tender—M, F, 1964
Young at Heart—M, F, 1965-66
Young Blood (Parts I and II)—M, F, 1965-66
Young Bulls, The—2BM, F, 1964-66

Young Couple (A)—M, F, 1946-47
(*Young Couple*) (B)—*Twelve Different Ways*
Young Couple (C)—M, F, England, 1966-67
Young Girl Lost—M, 2F, England, 1968
(*Young Hiker, The*)—*Modern Hitch Hiker, A*
Young Lovers—M, F, England, 1968
Young Lust—M, 2F, England, 1968
Young Movement—2M, 3F, 1968-70
(*Your* [sic] *Not Going to Stick That in Me*)—*Honeymoon, The*
(*You've Had It*)—*First Date*
Yum Yum Girl—M, BF, 1963-65

Zorba the Greek—2M, F, 1965-66
Zorro's Girls—2F, 1965-66

Al Di Lauro
is a New York painter and collagist who has had sixteen one-man shows, four in New York City. A long-time collector of stag materials, he made a feature film, *Old, Borrowed and Stag*, from stags from the 1920s and 1930s. The film is currently being distributed in the United States and Canada.

Gerald Rabkin
is a professor of theatre arts at Rutgers University in New Jersey. He has worked professionally as an actor and director and has written extensively on theatre and film for various journals and newspapers. He is the author of *Drama and Commitment: Politics in the American Theatre of the Thirties*.

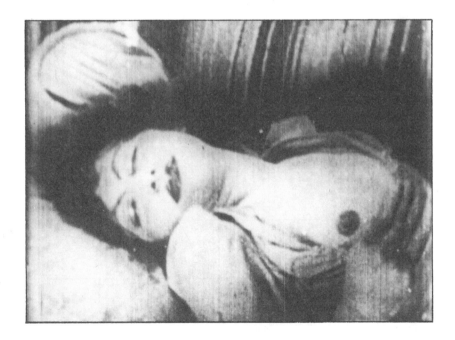

160

Bare Interlude, 1928-33.